Mrs. Alexander Fraser

Not While She Lives

A Novel: Vol. I.

Mrs. Alexander Fraser

Not While She Lives
A Novel: Vol. I.

ISBN/EAN: 9783337066468

Printed in Europe, USA, Canada, Australia, Japan

Cover: Foto ©Andreas Hilbeck / pixelio.de

More available books at **www.hansebooks.com**

NOT WHILE SHE LIVES.

NOT WHILE SHE LIVES.

A Novel.

BY

MRS. ALEXANDER FRASER,

AUTHOR OF "FAITHLESS," ETC.

"Omnia vincit Amor,
Et nos cedamus amori."

IN TWO VOLUMES.

VOL. I.

LONDON:

TINSLEY BROTHERS. 18, CATHERINE STREET, STRAND.

1870.

LONDON:
SAVILL, EDWARDS AND CO., PRINTERS, CHANDOS STREET,
COVENT GARDEN.

CONTENTS

OF

THE FIRST VOLUME.

Prologue.

NOT WHILE SHE LIVES.

PROLOGUE.

PART I.

" THOSE WHOM GOD HATH JOINED TOGETHER
LET NO MAN PUT ASUNDER."

 HE morning of an autumnal day.

Not in the bright and sunny South, with a turquoise sky above, with perpetual bloom to feast the eye, and "odours from Paradise" in the soft lambent air.

Nor amidst spreading ancestral trees, standing in friendly clumps, wreathing their giant forms and arms closely together; nor amongst lovely flower-bounded lanes and grassy dells, with the November sunshine slanting athwart the branches overhead, tinging all around with a deep and golden gleam, turning the variegated foliage of red and green and brown into rich mellow burnished shades, that seem all aglow and a-fire; falling upon sheaves of yellow ripe-eared corn; kissing the ruddy, luscious cheeks of the orchard fruit; shedding its genial beams on the distant undulating landscape, and deluding us into the belief that the glorious summer is still lingering with us, loth to leave the earth, whom its presence makes so fair.

But an autumnal morning in London.

Bitter as the blasts of adversity: cold as

the hard world's sympathy. No matter where the eye looked, not a speck of blue was discernible in the heavens; nothing but big sullen banks of heavy opaque clouds, with but a few sickly glimmers of sunlight struggling through the misty haze, adding, by their very unsuccessful efforts at emancipation, a duller and greyer tint, if possible, to everything. Moisture was the prevailing characteristic of the temperature. Not honest rain-drops, pattering down defiantly and boldly, but a sneaky, pitiful sort of Scotch mist, more felt than seen, exuding upon the irregular roof-tops, imparting a greasy appearance to the leads and slates, turning the mire of the roadway into a slushy liquid, resembling shoe-blacking, trickling sluggishly down area railings, and rendering the pavement physically dangerous.

1—2

Very few pedestrians were to be seen, however, voluntarily exposing themselves to the cold and damp that were part and parcel of the inclement weather; and, the few that *were* visible consisted chiefly of that class stigmatized very justly as the " great unwashed :" coal-heavers, sweeps with ebon physiognomies, navvies, and such like, were loafing about, all more or less with grimy, ill-looking visages, and remarkably unpleasant exteriors.

The dwellings on either side of the street bore upon them a corresponding stamp; consisting of poverty-stricken houses, with a patch of black clay in front, enclosed by dilapidated railings, and of which " chickweed" was the sole produce and adornment.

The locality in question was, in fact, one of the lowest and most disreputable suburbs of the metropolis. A dangerous quarter, especially at dusk, within which poverty and crime herded familiarly together, and huddled closely and lovingly with squalor and rags, rearing their Hydra heads an-tagonistically against all that savoured of affluence or respectability; a quarter infested with noisome human vermin, in the shape of night-birds, pickpockets, and out-casts; and owning, as its chief aristocracy, unshorn, unkempt Hebrews, itinerant vendors of periwinkles and cowheel; cats'-meat men, and elderly females with formidable biceps and weather-battered faces, diligently guarding their apple-stalls against the impudent depredations of myriads of street arabs, the incorrigible "gamins" that sloped in dozens about the place, in a perpetual state of revolutionism, crying, *una voce*, "*Liberté, Egalité, Frater-*

nité!" or collected in noisy belligerent masses on the adjacent door-steps.

Now and then, even at that early hour of the day, for it was barely 9 A.M., out of the half-ajar door of a gin palace reeled the form of some woman, with dishevelled hair and torn garments, and strong pugilistic tendencies visibly swelling in her breast, judging from the pugnacious glances she gave each passing individual, with a defiant imbecility in her look. Within the precincts of the " publics" glimpses of red could be caught, adorning the backs of the gallant defenders of our country, zealously performing their matutinal devotions to the Bacchanalian Deity. But, notwithstanding all the uninviting sights and sounds, and salient objections to the spot, the suburb yet boasted, in company with higher and sweller quarters, refuges for the sick, the vicious, the homeless, and the devotee.

It possessed its exact and proper quantum of hospitals, penitentiaries, reformatories, workhouses, police stations, and, above all other boons, a great big church—a church presenting no claim to any sort of architectural beauty, but standing out square and solid, and having as its sole ornament a painted window, whose subject was the parable of the "Good Samaritan," about the most appropriate device it could have had, considering the evil locality on which it looked. Through the richly-stained panes, the daylight shone in dimly, leaving in almost undistinguishable gloom, the lengthy aisles and the surrounding pews. A few waxen tapers faintly lit up the altar, the silver hair and white surplice of its officiating minister, and the rusty garments of the assisting clerk, and showed, sharply defined against the pervading darkness of the body of the large building, a group of four persons standing before the altar rails.

The responses were firmly uttered by the two principal actors in the scene, and the clergyman's solemn voice fell impressively and distinctly on the silent church:

"Those whom God hath joined together let no man put asunder."

Then came, in due course, the final blessing concluding the rites that bound indissolubly together two human beings, until death, ruthless, omnipotent, should come to divide them. The names of the wedded couple were duly registered, the customary fees bestowed, and "Mark Leslie," as he had just subscribed himself,

clasped his bride passionately in his arms,
and whispered loving words into her ear;
then saying, audibly, "At ten to-night,
Lucy," he hurriedly traversed the aisle,
and gaining the door was speedily lost to
view. Meanwhile the trio that he had left
behind him pursued their way more
slowly, in an opposite direction to the one
he had taken.

A strange looking bridal party it was!
not only curious from the peculiarity of
its proceedings, but from its incongruous
appearance; there was an amount of in-
congruity about it, in fact, that could not
have failed to attract observation from the
most indifferent and casual witness; but
the principal " looker on" had been the
minister, an aged man, wearily overworked
in this densely crowded parish, that was
rife with every species of vice, and requir-

ing for its amelioration infinite supervision, spiritual ministration and the utmost zealous attention.

A good old plodding man, labouring always indefatigably in the service of the Great Master, and unselfishly and unmurmuringly sacrificing every material comfort to the one desire and hope of his true Christianly life, that of furthering, to the utmost of his humble but honest ability, the welfare of immortal souls. He had long ago "renounced the devil and all his works, the pomps and vanities of a wicked world, and all the sinful lusts of the flesh," for a pure life of devotion to Heaven and his suffering fellow creatures: he was a holy man and no Pharisee; thoroughly simple; somewhat obtuse, perhaps; and no scrutinizer or meddler into things that concerned him not.

The bridegroom was a mere stripling,
over whose head not more than nineteen
summers at most could have rolled their
course, judging from the slight boyishness
of his tall, lithe figure, and the clear fresh-
ness of colouring that belongs especially
to extreme youth. He bore upon him an
unmistakeable impress of patrician breeding
in the wonderful delicacy of his chiselled
features, and the refinement that distinguished his *tout ensemble.*

The bride was his complete anti-
thesis.

In spite of the halo of romance and
interest that might have naturally been
inspired in a beholder by the pure white
dress, and symbolical orange-blossoms that
shone above her braids, and that enhanced
her attractions, and "elevated" her appearance as much as art could do, "ple-

beianism" stamped her undeniably for its own. And yet she could boast of a certain gorgeousness of beauty that many a fair aristocrat would have envied, and been willing to barter some of her *sang azul* for. A beauty that was almost too bright and blooming and bewildering, in fact, in its tints and sensuousness; resplendent in a warm " morbidezza" of colour and ruddy wealths of hair, gleaming bronze in the sunlight; almond - shaped " love-darting " eyes, like those of an Eastern houri, but of a deep dark grey, thickly fringed on upper and lower lid by black curling lashes, and with green peculiar coruscations glancing rapidly every now and then across the large pupils; full "vermeil-tinctured" lips, beautifully curved and slightly drooping at the corners; a complexion that presented an exquisite mixture of snow with Provence roses, save where a few freckles tanned the fair face, and marked a little strongly the formation of the cheek-bones, that were too prominent for preserving the exact lines of the oval countenance, and which denoted her north-country origin.

She had a well-developed form, too, inclining to massiveness about the white throat and shoulders. Her hands, though tightly compressed in gloves, showed masculine dimensions; and her feet, in their new bronze *chaussure*, displayed far greater utility for exercise than Cendrillon proportions. .

Her voice, and her constantly recurring laugh, as she conversed with her companions, sounded loud and rather discordant; and her accents would have grated on, and irritated any delicately-sensitive

ear, whilst there was a something inde-
finable—a little "uncanny" perhaps, as
the Scotch have it—in the broad smiles
that parted her full lips, giving to view
a set of large, strong, but very white
teeth.

Her male attendant was habited in
rather a peculiar and original fashion
for a ceremonial of matrimony. A shabby
claret-coloured coat, profusely adorned by
big brass buttons, which had evidently
been intended primarily for an individual
double his size, and which must have been
an investment from a slop-shop, where it
had probably been left in pledge by an
indigent flunkey, hung in loose unseemly
folds upon his slim figure, wiry as a ter-
rier's. An almost napless hat, with a
broad brim that was funnily erratic here
and there, was drawn closely down over

his deeply-wrinkled forehead, and a dingy woollen comforter, or *cache nez*, enveloped three or four times his lean and sallow neck, and concealed almost the whole of the lower portion of his physiognomy. What *could* be seen of his visage was unprepossessing to the highest degree, leaving no desire for further investigation of his features.   Slyness and cunning twinkled in the eyes that age, or a perpetual state of intoxication, had divested of any pristine colour, leaving an ugly opaqueness about the ball, and a bleary and neutral tint about the pupils, in which, however, a close observer might have detected the same greenish lights now and then, as were discernible in the wondrous orbs of his daughter.

But with this one strange resemblance about the eyes, all imaginable likeness

ceased entirely between them.   He was
as repulsive and ill-looking a specimen of
the human race as she was the reverse.

The woman who formed the trio, and
whom the bride sometimes designated as
" Granny," appeared to be a sort of
dummy or nonentity.   She wore an appearance of dotage, but a dotage that was
repellant to look upon, instead of presenting an aspect of childishness or helpless-
ness.   As she hobbled along with difficulty,
endeavouring to keep pace with the others,
her head and hands seemed affected with
a slight tremulous movement, suggestive
of palsy, or an overdue affection for strong
waters, like her son.   Her eyes had a
vacant wandering turn; and her thin lips,
tightly compressed together from paucity
of teeth, showed a curious *rapprochement* of
the olfactory organ with her pointed chin.

Walking leisurely along, the bride carefully guarding her wedding garments from speck or soil, the trio at length turned into a low public-house, over which hung a flaunting signboard, inscribed in huge yellow letters,

"THE LION AND THE MOUSE."

Above these words there appeared in coarse vivid tints an illustrative design of the same, representing a small and meek-looking animal of a purely imaginative species, writhing within the paw of a larger one, equally puzzling in definition, and in the portrayal of which conflict some amateur limner had evidently essayed to give to the world at large, a mild and remarkably original specimen of his uncultured talents.

The party on entering seated themselves, and the claret-clad man vociferated loudly for refreshment.

"A pint of bitter," he called out, impatiently, to the "buxom party," who was busy as a bee amongst the shoals of drones who buzzed round the bar, over the foaming tankards of creamy porter and ale. ·

"Look sharp, girl!" he reiterated. "I am as dry as a bone after my morning's work; and a fine morning's work it has been too!" he chuckled, rubbing his meagre hands together, and winking slyly at his daughter as he emptied the draught at one pull.

"This is poor stuff to wet one's throat with on such an occasion. Ain't you going to stand nothing, Lucy? I saw the fine gent slip some yellow shiners into your hand on leaving you. Fork 'em out, lass, and don't be close-fisted! Why, damme, you must be liberal, like a *real* lady, now that you *are* one!"

"Of course you saw the gold, Father! Sure their glitter wasn't likely to escape *your* eyes! But my money is my own, and if I *have* married a 'fine gent' to become a fine lady, it concerns only myself. It wont go far towards making you respectable—or honest even, I am afraid! I am not a going to be bullied, I'll swear!" she added, in a dogged, sulky tone, while the grey eyes flashed up greenly, and the large white teeth were determinedly set together.

"However, I don't wish a row to-day, Father, so call for what you want and I'll pay. Let us have gin, 'neat — what Granny likes, you know—and we'll drink Mr. Mark Leslie's health in it. Such a

nice, sweet spoken gentleman as he is, and
so good at book learning; but for all that
I am the cleverer of the two, I'll warrant!"
and she laughed loudly.

"And when is he coming for you? I
am not near, as I knows of, in my ways;
but I am a very poor man, working hard to
get my daily bread, and hardly managing
to keep myself in victuals at all," the old
hypocrite whimpered out querulously,
trying to force up a tear into his eyes, and
entirely forgetting that his two companions
were up to his tricks and shams.

"It *is* a shame if I am to keep you any
longer; but you'll give me somethink a
week, wont you, *dear?*" he coaxed in a
wheedling voice, with avarice shining out
of every feature of his face.

He was a man that could hardly have
resisted selling his soul for the sum of

half-a-crown, if the would-be purchaser had held out the coin glitteringly and temptingly before him. Avariciousness and cunning were the component parts of his character. The avariciousness of a Jew, the "cunning which is the usual substitute that the really low and uneducated classes have for wisdom."

"A small matter of ten bob a week, Lu; a trifle, considering that you are that particular in your eating, turning up your nose at good meat, and fancying shrimps and cresses, and such like. No; I don't think I am asking too much—I don't indeed!"

"Well, well, Father, I'll see about it; make your mind easy, and don't go a whimpering and a fretting like an old woman. Why, even Granny isn't so stupid. Be a man and you'll earn something; but

you will always be a begging of others if
you go on shilly-shally, doing nothing but
drink, drink! And now listen to me:
Mind you have something decent for
supper to-night, for Robert is coming."

"Robert—Robert Minton! Are you
gone crazy, girl? Do you forget already
that this is your marriage-day? For
shame, to see your old sweetheart when
you should have thoughts for your husband
only!"

"Just hold your tongue, *will* you!" she
snapped out so sharply and angrily that
the man settled into silence at once.
"Husbands be hanged, I say! Nothing
nor nobody will ever come between Robert
and me! Do you think, you foolish old
man, that I care a rush for the whey-faced
boy that has married me for my pretty
looks? Come along, do, and don't stop

chattering here about things that you understand nothing about; and if you do,
they don't concern you. Why, Father!"
and she burst into a hoarse merriment as
she looked him impudently and jeeringly
in the face, " I am sure the world must be
coming to an end, when *you*, above all
people, try and come the respectable and
virtuous dodge!"

PART II.

"TILL DEATH US DO PART."

"For the lips of a strange woman drop as an honey-comb, and her mouth is smoother than oil, but her end is bitter as wormwood, sharp as a two-edged. sword."—*Proverbs of Solomon.*

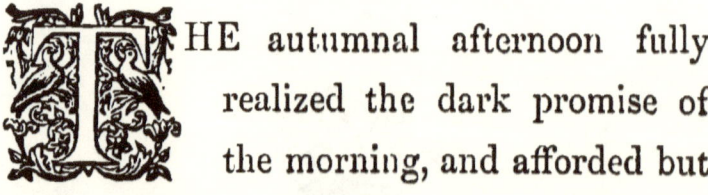HE autumnal afternoon fully realized the dark promise of the morning, and afforded but a dreary look out to the occupants of a row of small-sized houses that presented a façade that was all vulgar stucco and bright green railings.

They lay in an out-of-the-way and unfashionable locality, somewhere in the vicinity of the New Road, and rejoiced in the mellifluous sounding appellation of " Mandeville Terrace," to which address the more aspiring of their proprietors affixed the imposing addition of " York Gate."

At No. 8, with his face closely pressed up against the small square window-pane, stood an old gentleman of some three score years and ten; and whilst he stood there as immovable as though he were a statue, or in a photographic *pose*, it could be seen at a glance that he was both aristocratic and pleasant looking in his green old age, owning a pair of mild blue eyes, full of serenity, and a face replete with goodness; with a fine expanse of brow that Lavater would have rejoiced in, and a mouth rife with an expression of amiability. He was

apparently the sole and undisputed occupant of the diminutive and somewhat
dingy parlour to which the window apper-
tained. His wife had been laid in the
churchyard that was many a hundred mile
distant from the metropolis, some dozen
years and more, but he had remained in
solitary blessedness, mostly for the sake of
the all-absorbing affection he had for an
only son, and partly from the fact that no
" damsel withering on the stalk" had been
thrown in his path possessing sufficient
attraction, either personally or mentally, to
induce him to launch the barque of life a
second time on the ordinarily stormy waves
of the matrimonial ocean.

It was, however, no evil or unfortunate
experience of marriage that had deterred
him from reassuming the Benedict's yoke,
for the dead partner of his bosom had been

a pattern woman, a model to the feminine sex; a sensible, thrifty housewife, full of domestic virtues, rigid principles, and a fund of inexhaustible good temper, although she was perhaps somewhat humdrum in her ways, and sometimes provokingly wearisome in her clockwork punctuality and unflagging attention to the petty diurnal duties of homely life.

She was, however, a woman who could scarcely have failed in her endeavours to render any man happy, or what would be a more appropriate term, "comfortable," provided always that she had been allowed to insure comfort to him in her own commonplace, matter-of-fact fashion, and provided also that he was of the *genus homo* who are not too *exigeant* in disposition, inclined to cavil querulously at fidgety trivialities, and requiring something a little sparkling and *spirituelle* in the daily companion of their days.

The poor deceased lady had had the uncommon luck in this world, where marriage is often the antipodes of Heaven, to pitch upon just the right man to suit her, out of a host of aspirants to her favour, or to the *beaux yeux de sa cassette*, for she had been a spinster of independent means, with sufficient in the funds to make her an heiress in a small way.

She had sensibly selected the worthiest of her suitors, having, with the judgment of an experienced lapidary, discovered the real "jew's eye" amidst the meretricious mass of paste offered to her acceptance; and she never regretted her choice, for her chosen spouse proved to be lenient to her shortcomings on the score of accomplishments, requiring only the qualities essential to forming a true gentlewoman; and the pair glided on smoothly and glibly enough in connubial harness, never "kicking over the traces," until it pleased Providence to sever them.

After she had left his side for ever, instead of rushing with avidity into the pleasures of new-found freedom, and bachelor licence, he would stay at home, and catch himself recalling with emotion the plurality of virtues the lamented defunct had possessed, and would find himself, from force of habit, occasionally listening for the well-known clicking of her knitting-needles —knitting having been an occupation in which she had delighted during her lifetime. He missed the queries, reiterated each evening with little or no variance in their mode of fashioning, as to the welfare of his cattle, the sanitary condition and growth of his potato and turnip crops, the flourishing state of his mangel-wurzel, the foaling of his mares, and the success of any new-fangled patents, in the shape of churns and other domestic utilities.

For the lodger at No. 8, Mandeville Terrace, had, in the halcyon times gone by, been what is termed a gentleman-farmer, not exactly opulent, but decidedly well-to-do in the world. He had ventured upon the stream of speculation, not rashly and thoughtlessly, but quietly, with prudence presiding at the helm; and speculation had turned out favourably, allowing him to indulge to a moderate extent in a long-standing hobby he had had for agricultural pursuits.

Beechwood Grange was the name of the old place, half house, half cottage ornée, in which he had first seen the light, and

to which he had taken his bride, and it
was a spot to be justly proud of—a gem
of prettiness, though its beauties were of
a microscopical nature; but although the
whole thing was tiny and slightly dollish,
it was wonderfully well kept outwardly,
and the interior arrangements corre-
sponded in comfort.

The house rejoiced in a small model
farm, replete with all the modern inven-
tions of the Eastern and Western hemi-
spheres. Some that were as mysterious
in principle as they were useless in trial;
and others that worked admirably, saving
an immensity of time, expense, and manual
labour.

The grounds were more shrubbed than
wooded; but from them could be easily
discerned, on a fine day, by the naked eye,
the outline of the lovely Malvern Hills

rearing themselves against the clear bright sky.

A shallow streamlet ran purling through the extremity of the grounds, and across it oaks, elms, and other forest trees, but all more or less saplings, waved their arms and nodded their heads familiarly to each other, in acknowledgment of each revivifying breeze. Down in the depths of the water any disciple of Izaac Walton would have found himself amply rewarded for his trouble, by heavy hauls of the smaller species of the finny tribe.

A rough and rustic boat-house was erected at one end of the fairy bank, and a miniature craft, fit for the " Lady of the Lake," was moored close by.

In winter time, when the young trees that nodded and waved, grew leafless and gaunt-armed, casting queer shadows upon the water—when depths and depths of white snow laid far out of sight all the exquisite floral ornaments of Mother Earth —when the hoar frost hung on each shrub like diamonds, and gave with a sharp crackle under the human footfall—when the temperature set in due north from the Arctic regions, as it were—then great fires blazed cheerily away, and Beechwood Grange "within" became lively with guests and Christmas festivities, and each comfortable nook and corner were resonant with ringing voices and merry laughter.

But all this was now long gone by.

The light of other days had faded; the tide of fortune had flowed in once plenteously, but had ebbed away again.

The gigantic "Steadfast" Bank suddenly stopped payment, and whilst some few were heavy losers by the crash, hundreds were irretrievably ruined.

Amongst the former category, however, the Squire of Beechwood fortunately ranked.

Almost in the twinkling of an eye, however, he had turned from downright prosperity, if not into absolute poverty, at any rate into a state bearing, in comparison with his former life, a close resemblance to it. Still he had escaped with a small sum, sufficient to keep his head out of the water that had completely engulphed scores of his fellow sufferers.

Just twelve months after his wife's death, the house in which she had drawn her last breath was, with all its costly adjuncts, sold to the highest bidder; and the widower, with a strangely wistful look in his poor eyes, and a quiver upon his lip, bade a mournful farewell to the pleasant scenes that had known him in more prosperous hours, and, accompanied by his son, located himself in the dwelling where we find him.

To a discontented and rebellious spirit, painful and irritating to excess would have been the wonderful contrast between the old life and the new one—between the well-remembered sunny aspect of the Grange, with all its elegances and super-fluities, and the miserable poky domicile that had everything so essentially vulgar and cockneyfied about it, with an aggravating apology for a garden in a few feet of London mud, stuck over primly and formally in staring semi - circles and straight lines, with half a dozen sickly, insipid Sweet-Williams, some atrociously

odoriferous Marigolds, and one or two
flaunting Hollyhocks defiantly parading
their garish hues on high.

But the poor old gentleman possessed
the attributes of the "noble army of
martyrs"—patience and resignation to God's
will were his chief characteristics. He had
never been of a grumbling or mutinous
turn, but rather of a religious disposition,
and now he bowed himself meekly and
uncomplainingly to the state of life to
which Heaven had called him.

In the midst of his terribly *statu-quo*
existence, he found, *faute de mieux*, a mild
sort of excitement and gratification in tend-
ing and doctoring with infinite care the
few unhealthy specimens of floriculture
that struggled on for life within his circum-
scribed parterre, and he felt an enlivenment
during the solitary hours which his son's

absence in the City entailed upon him, in the puny and rather spasmodical chirp of a pale, fluffy canary that perpetually molted in a bright brass cage near the window.

On the particular afternoon in question, his son's absence had evidently been prolonged beyond the customary hour, judging by the quick searching glances that the mild blue eyes shot out into the dark prospect, as they peered just above the wire blind, as though in quest of some one.

At length hurried footsteps resounded on the narrow pavement, and nodding pleasantly to his father, the absentee entered the house.

" You are late, my boy ! I have been watching for you, fearing something unusual must have occurred to detain you so much beyond your time. What delayed you ?"

A third party, had one been present, could scarcely have failed in noticing a vivid accession of colour that flamed up into the truant's cheek, as the question was put, although it was easy to perceive that there had been no ulterior motive in its asking, and that it scarcely even enforced a reply, for now that his son *had* returned safe and sound in limb, the old gentleman was experiencing no feeling in his mind but one of perfect contentment, and whilst he spoke he was occupied in leisurely drawing a wrapper over the brass birdcage, to insure comfort and cosiness to his feathered companion during his night's siesta.

"Very sorry to be so late, Father, but I had a little surplus work to get through to-day. Have you been alone all the time?"

"No, your uncle Gresham called and sat with me over an hour. By-the-bye, you know that girl whom you picked up insensible after her fall out of the cart ?"

"Yes! Father; *what* of her?" was asked, breathlessly.

"I fancied from your description of her, that she was too superior a person to be left to such worthless surroundings as you represented her people to be. Now, though I have not much, yet, God be thanked! I have still enough money left, to do good in a small way. And thinking your uncle a shrewd sensible fellow, I commissioned him to make inquiries, determining to find some lady friend who would take the girl into service, or get her employed some way, to keep her out of harm; provided, of course, that the report was satisfactory; to-day he brought me the result of his investigations, and from the very reliable sources from whence he derived his

information, I am inclined to think his
account a correct one."

"Well, Father!" And the young fellow's
eye lit up with the prospect of hearing
that the being he so passionately loved was
simply perfection—a modern Griselda, in
fact—brimming over with every imaginable
virtue, and, for the very first time in his
iife, an undutiful impatience rose up in his
breast at "the dear old governor's habitua
prosiness."

"Gresham says, she is lovely, but worthless! It appears that she earns a trifling
stipend as a serio-comic vocalist at one of
the minor and most disreputable music
halls in Islington, 'The Aspasian Pavilion;' and all her gains are spent on a
great lazy rascal, who ought to have
married her long ago to have made an
honest woman of her. Your uncle saw

him by chance, and describes him as a showy, bold style of fellow, with a heavy beard. The other inmates of the house where the Wellands lodge, assert that the man and the girl have been together, off and on, for a couple of years. Have you ever seen him?"

" Yes, Father; I really don't know," stammered the boy, incoherently.

" A showy man, with a heavy beard—the same, my God! in whose arms I caught her but two days ago, and she swore to me that he was her brother!" he murmured to himself, with cold beads of perspiration starting on his brow, and his cheek of an ashen hue.

A blow from a feather would have knocked him down as he tried to stand up and walk a few steps, but was forced to relinquish the attempt from sheer inability

to steady his trembling limbs; neither
could he venture to articulate when the
words seemed to be gurgling and dying
away in his throat.

By this time the old gentleman having
arranged the covering of the cage satisfac-
torily to himself, had hung it up, then re-
adjusting his spectacles, he prepared to seat
himself for his evening repast. Turning,
he noted at a glance the strange drawn
look of utter misery that was visible on
every feature of the face he loved.

At once paternal anxiety roused up visions
of illness! danger of all kinds threatening
the object so dear to him, the only object
for whose sake he prayed Heaven daily
and nightly to spin out a little longer the
span of his own existence—loomed before
his alarmed imagination, and made him ex-
claim, in nervous accent—

"What *is* the matter! Are you ill?"

"Nothing, sir; nothing!" But the words fell slowly and with some difficulty, and the languid tone gave a direct denial to his assertion.

"Over tired; or the weather, perhaps! Do not alarm yourself so, Father. I'll go upstairs and lie down quietly a bit, and shall soon be myself again!" he added, calling up a ghost of a smile to his lip, and then dragging himself wearily up the stairs, he reached his room, and, locking the door, flung himself down to think.

"To think!" a sad and dreary task at best, when "thoughts" in this world of woe so much oftener wear for us a painful and ofttimes even an unbearable aspect, than a pleasant one.

The boy tried to call his bewildered

thoughts together, that he might reflect on
the course of action he should pursue;
but in that moment of rough and rude
awakening from his most delicious dream,
revenge the fiercest upon her, hatred the
most implacable towards his rival, were
the two turbulent passions that filled his
breast, and yet "he that studieth revenge
keepeth his own wounds green," and he
felt that what he wanted most of all in
his first hour of desolation, was balm to
heal his stricken soul, not caustic to irritate
his wounds.

He knew full well that all his hopes were
blighted almost ere they had blossomed;
that the flowers of his life were scattered
away ruthlessly, before his hand had
thoroughly grasped them; that all faith in,
and respect for human nature were blasted
in his eyes "for ever."

It was not likely in that bitter moment that he should believe that his suffering was but transitory after all; that "for ever" is a phrase often used, but rarely meant, seldom finding a genuine echo in the heart unless for a transient period; that it is ordinarily but an expression on the lips, or a chimera of a sick brain; that, in fact, everything in this life, be it joy or sorrow, love, faith, revenge, or hatred, are but fleeting and passing, as the winged wind; that *nothing* endures but for a season.

All that he *could* realize was that his whole future was wrecked—stranded irremediably; that nothing but immeasurable misery awaited him—misery either way—whether he was with her, knowing her to be utterly false; misery without her, for he adored her madly still!

In spite of all—in the face of confidence and affection both betrayed and basely outraged, and his honour arraigned—the very pangs of jealousy that seemed to be rending his soul in twain, were in them- selves sure and irrefragable proofs that his love for her still lived vigorously as ever; he was convinced that as long as existence lasted, her loss would leave a horrible va- cuum in his heart that it would be im- possible for anyone on earth to fill up, for he worshipped her with the fierce unreasoning passion of youth; and it would have seemed to him a desecration of his own feelings to imagine that that love was not love after all, but only the ephemera of an hour.

That in fact what he doated on, was not " *her*," but a being of his own creation, clothed in the bright beauty that had dazzled him, and made him sacrifice all to make it his own.

Oh! how like cruel fiends those words "his own," in conjunction with her, seemed to mock at him with their meaning; to laugh him to scorn for his absurd credulity!

It was galling indeed to his pride to have been fooled so entirely—to have swallowed with avidity all her specious assurances, as though they had been an "honeycomb," but to find them "wormwood" at the last—to have craved, yearned for tenderness from her, only to have met a more cruel thrust than that of a "two-edged sword."

To have been rivalled by a low, uneducated ruffian, to whom she had assuredly all along belonged, whilst she was persuading her "husband," her poor deluded victim, by the power of her beauty and blandishments, to believe her true as steel, and pure as the undriven snow!

In one of Juvenal's Satires are found the words, "None become at once completely vile;" but just as "men may rise on stepping-stones of their dead selves to higher things," so they often slip and slip, surely but slowly, down to the lowest depths.

"She must be innately bad and base," he reflected; for, young as he was in worldly wisdom, he yet possessed sufficient sense to know that deliberate vice—vice perpetrated in cold blood—is neither a gourd nor a mushroom, springing up rapidly in the course of a few hours, to be eradicated by a simple effort and destroyed entirely by a blow.

It is rather a poisonous fungus, implanted early in the heart, fostered in its growth and strength by that heart's own human tendency to evil, and requiring strenuous exertion and unlimited patience to pluck it out root by root; but a patience outlasting Penelope's—a patience rare and scarcely attainable, and that can best be exemplified by the old Arabian aphorism, " Be patient, and the mulberry-leaf will turn into satin!"

" Can such falsity really exist ? or is it but a hideous nightmare after all?" he questioned himself. His uncle was a cynical man of the world, sceptical of goodness and worth. Could his judgment have been swayed by the fabrications of those, to whom a shilling was sufficient inducement to "speak," and whose natural bent was falsehood more than truth ? But no shadow of a loophole by which his

query might meet with contradiction presented itself, and with his young heart
swelling high under the sense of his bitter
wrong, all that he longed for was to lie
down and die!

After all, he was but nineteen years
of age, and the fortitude and strength
of manhood were terribly incomplete in
his nature. He was trying to grapple
with a grief, the magnitude of which
would have overwhelmed many a man
of riper age.

Poor fellow! he had let himself, with the
folly and recklessness of an inexperienced
swimmer, float carelessly down the river
of life, and he had not even tried to
evade, in his headlong career, any shoals
that might endanger the passage. All of
a sudden he had reached the tempestuous
ocean, with breakers ahead of him, with

the tide of fate running strongly against him, with huge waves of sorrow rising around him, and it was "too late" even to try and find a haven of safety. Ah! what had he done to be drifted into such a doom? There was nothing left for him now—no chance of rescue from the wreck of everything that could yield happiness to him upon this earth.

> " The miserable have no other medicine
> But only Hope."

And even that was denied him at present. Hope, the "salve of life," which in most cases comes to lighten the gloom of a desponding heart; for it is a merciful dispensation of Providence that in this world, " whose brightest visions of felicity prove to be but a shadow of a shade; whose past pleasures, whilst they feast memory, yet leave the heart aching with

4—2

a sense of their desertion; and whose present enjoyments vanish and wither almost
before they bloom;" that the more en-
during sentiment of "Hope" is given to
keep up a sinking spirit.

Do we not read that when Sin entered
the bowers of Paradise, and the primal
curse drove Adam and Eve from the
garden of glowing delights, that it was
"Hope," called by the ancients the off-
spring of untarnished joys, who took
up his abode with the wretched exiles
of Eden, and preserved them from despair?

But Hope only comes when the first
fresh poignancy of grief has passed away,
although the glimmer of its advent has
unconsciously been the sole light that has
saved many a human being from the
crime of self-destruction.

A thought struck the suffering boy, and he started.

He had married her under a feigned name! Not from any premeditated deceit, or desire to play her false, but simply from a concatenation of circumstances. He had given her a *nom de guerre* on first acquaintance. just on the spur of the moment, but with no shadow of an *arrière pensée* in doing so, and later he had lacked the courage to reveal the fraud; but his conscience had scarcely blamed the deception, for his purpose towards her had ever been true and honest.

Legally, then, he wondered, would his secret marriage be invalid? and he free— free as the wanton wind—released from the now loathsome bonds in which the words of a priest had a few hours before fettered him? But as he pondered

anxiously upon this, there came ringing
through his brain, just like a dirge for
the death of his momentary hope, the
good old man's slow and solemn injunc-
tion—"Those whom God hath joined together let no man put asunder."   Perhaps
if he had been older, or harder, more a
denizen of the world, those few words
would have failed in producing the same
effect upon him as they did now.

But he was young, enthusiastic, religious; no impulse to mock at them entered
his mind; but rather there came over him
a sort of impetuous desire for self-sacrifice,
sooner than that they should be treated
as if unspoken, and their meaning hurled
to the four winds, just for the sake of mere
earthly feelings and wishes.

"No!" he cried, fervently, throwing
himself down on his knees; "she *is* my

wife in the sight of God, if not in the
sight of men. Great Heaven! that looked
down on my vows, hear me whilst I swear
that not while she lives shall word or act
of mine sever the tie that binds us together, 'for better, for worse'! 'to love and
to cherish'! '*till death us do part*'! Oh, *why,
why* have you deceived me so, my darling!
my darling!—I, who would have loved
and cherished you all my life!" The big
tears rushed to his eyes again and again,
in spite of his efforts to dash them away;
and just as if to add the last drop to his
already overflowing cup of misery, cruel
memory recalled with tenacious vividness
the face of the woman he had so longed
to clasp—the glorious tints of hair that
had floated in ruddy luxuriance over
his arms, and been pressed frantically
in boyish fervour to his beating heart

and quivering lips—the strangely beautiful eyes—the ruby, enticing mouth, that had uttered that very day, oaths that he had deemed in all faith to be so loyal and so true!

"I will try and nerve myself to my fate, but I dare not look upon her again," he said at last resolutely; and rising from his dejected attitude, he drew pen and ink to his side. "I will write and say I know *all*—that she and I can never, *never* meet again upon earth! And then good-bye to my miserable past—away into oblivion with everything! Oblivion, indeed! What a word. Can a convict ever find oblivion with the manacles tightly clasped on his limbs—with the loathsome chain clanging and dragging at his heels? Can the human breast rest in forgetfulness when everything around reminds it continually of what it has lost? And she was *all* to me!—brightness and sunshine, love and joy, all!—and the whole world will be a desert without her! Poets may prate idly of a Lethean stream, but prose owns no such mythical remedy. Alas! prose itself —real, downright prose—will, however, be the only cure for me. Thank God! she knows me as 'Mark Leslie' only, and I shall be spared her tracing me; to look upon her again and then to part would be a thousand times worse than death. My poor old father! if you only knew all, I believe you would break your heart—how your son has disgraced himself, dishonoured the old name, and bound himself, hand and foot, to a common 'music-hall' singer! That were nothing if she was but honest, but oh, my God! a mere light o' love— the worthless leman of a low-lived ruffian!"

PART III.

FOILED! FATHER.

" My life is cold, and dark, and dreary;
  It rains, and the wind is never weary.
    My thoughts still cling to the mouldering past,
    But the hopes of youth fall thick in the blast,
    And the days are dark and dreary !"
                                    Longfellow.

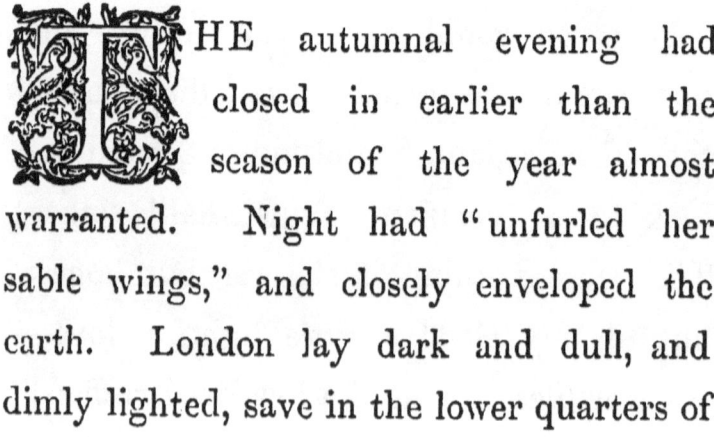

HE autumnal evening had closed in earlier than the season of the year almost warranted. Night had "unfurled her sable wings," and closely enveloped the earth. London lay dark and dull, and dimly lighted, save in the lower quarters of

the town, where petty traders plied incessantly and indefatigably on, far into the
hours in which the richer portions of the
working classes in the more fashionable
localities sought either rest or amusement.

At the door of a small and shabby-
looking house, situated in one of the back
streets of Islington, stood David Welland.
His well-worn coat, that had served him
as a marriage garment in the morning, now
shielded him, as effectually as its threadbare
texture would permit of, from the keen
blasts of wind that came howling and
moaning up the dirty pavement. The
same dingy comforter encircled his throat;
but the napless hat, that had probably been
carefully put by for another state ceremonial, was replaced by a woollen cap that
was faded, and had long ago seen its palmy

days, but which, though guarding his head
from cold, yet revealed far more conspicu-
ously than its predecessor had done the
workings of his countenance and the expression of his eyes, as he scanned anxiously
each approaching figure in the street, and
peered curiously into the face of each
passer-by.

In a room situated at the back of the
house, at whose entrance Welland had evidently "mounted guard," a gas-jet sent
down its yellow glare upon some fragments
of food, not over *recherché* in quality, that
remained in the blue earthenware dishes
that still adorned the festive board. An
empty pewter pot or two and a coarsely-
painted tobacco-jar stood also on the deal
table, on one end of which rested the
slovenly-shod feet of a man who lounged
negligently back in his chair. Through

the atmosphere, redolent of smoke, it could be distinguished that he was a man over whom some five and thirty years of a hard life had rolled. His almost herculean proportions, even in the half-reclining position he held, were such as to excite the utmost admiration and enthusiasm in the prizering, though in more refined circles, less bulkiness and more elegance would have been deemed very desirable. An immense breadth of chest showed up beneath the seedy brown velveteen coat, that was thrown open, displaying beneath it a coarse calico shirt, not over daintily white in hue, and with a pattern of large red horseshoes all over its surface; a sky-blue cravat, knotted loosely round his bull-neck, was passed through another horseshoe of red coral that glittered from under the hair of his beard. Trousers of a very large black and white check, extravagantly pegtop, and a thick gilt watch-chain, with a bunch of showy pendants attached to it, completed his attire.

He was a *Vaurien* A 1—a gaol-bird—a "jack of all trades, and master of none;" gaining his livelihood in any way that he could, and without being over scrupulous as to how, provided that the *way* required for him no particular amount of mental or bodily exertion. Sometimes a bookmaker at Epsom or Ascot, or a prompter at some suburban theatre; a horse-dealer in a petty way; a secretary to some Cold-Meat Association; an occasional speculator in rat-fights; and now and then even a temporary clerk at some church. He had a decent modicum of brain, which, if it had been properly cultivated, would have made him even a useful member of low life, instead of being what he was, a disgrace to the human species.

But a foundling and a mudlark, in infancy and boyhood, uncared for, and left to go his own gait without let or hindrance, riper years found him, as a matter of consequence, nothing but a thorough vagabond and a scamp.

A showy-looking scamp he was too, with big curly rings of coal-black hair, evidently iled and tended with care; bold features, but regular enough in outline, with a sort of reckless dare-devil expression in the dark defiant eyes, that yet shone with a considerable sharpness and intelligence. There was an unpleasant look hovering over the lips, between which a long, coarse clay pipe rested, out of which, as he leant back in his seat, he amused himself by carelessly blowing upwards to the low ceiling, voluminous

wreaths of tobacco smoke. His hands
were large and bony about the knuckles,
and not over clean, with one or two flashy
rings, with imitation rubies, ornamenting
his fingers. There was a very good show
of muscle in the arm, that was thrown indolently over the shoulder of a woman,
who crouched on her knees close by his
side, and looked lovingly up into his
face.

As she knelt there, the whole character
of her beauty was changed from the aspect
it had worn in the morning. The countenance seemed "spiritualized," as it were;
true, the gas lit up each luxuriant tress
until its red tint grew almost too ruddy,
and seemed to be all aglow and afire; but
the green coruscations in her pupils were
invisible, leaving the large grey eyes
under their long curling lashes perfect

wells of tenderness and truth. The vivid
colour that usually tinged her cheek had
paled to a more delicate rose blush, and
the full sensuous lips smiled with a pleasant and happy expression, as they kissed
repeatedly the hand that caressed her.

It was perfectly marvellous, the transformation that this man's presence made
in her appearance.

With all her faults, follies, and even
crimes—and their name was " Legion "—to
this one human being whom she adored
she was an angel, unselfish, self-sacrificing,
unswerving in her fealty. Ruffian and
blackguard though he was, and none of the
dark shades of his character were hidden
from her watchful jealous eye, she was
faithful to the death to her idol. So faithful, that if it had fallen into worthless
shivers at her feet, she would have stooped

and carefully gathered up the broken fragments, preserving them in her heart of
hearts as a million times more priceless to
her than images entire, unblemished, and
untarnished. She would have garnered up
each speck of dust, and treasured each tiny
atom of it as unbounded wealth. " In the
wildest anarchy of human nature's insur-
gent appetites and sins, there is usually
some reclaiming virtue."

Very few creatures in this world, be they
ever so innately coarse and low, and even
vicious, are so utterly brutal as not to
possess some one aspiration or sentiment,
better and purer than the rest, lurking
beneath a mass of evil, and lying dormant
end insensible, perhaps only from the fact
that no object has appeared upon the scene
possessing sufficient power to awaken the
better feeling into being.

All that this woman had of refinement —if such a term can be used—in her, was called forth by the tones and touch of the only creature she really cared for in the wide wide world, although his tones were generally of the roughest, and his touch full many a black action had defiled. She had but little wealth to spare ; nothing, indeed, but the scanty earnings she managed to scrape together at the poorly remunerative profession of singer at a music hall; and the "Aspasian Pavilion" being the resort of the scum of the earth, the proprietor's generosity was in keeping with the profits he was enabled to make out of a rough lot of navvies, far richer in bad language than in pocket.

But, nevertheless, though the sum was small, she gave it at once, freely and ungrudgingly, into her lover's hand, never dreaming of words of gratitude from him, and only too happy in the knowledge that she was conducing by her mite to his welfare and comfort.

In spite of her uneducated mind—in spite of all the gross and vulgar elements by which she was surrounded, and amidst which she had been both born and nur-tured—she shrank, with a refinement of delicacy that would have done honour to the grandest duchess in the land from any allusion, ever so covert, to the obligation he owed her for repeated pecuniary help during the period that they had known each other.

She would never have hesitated to starve herself to death unrepiningly, if by such means she could have insured com-petency to him for the remainder of his natural existence. And yet she knew full

well that his *ways* were not what even
she, in her somewhat lax notions of morality
and probity, approved of; but amidst all
his shortcomings and delinquencies, doubts
of his constancy to her had never arisen to
torture her soul. She felt *sure* of him,
and for the sake of that one virtue,
fidelity, his million vices were fully and
freely forgiven and forgotten.

"So, Lucy"—and he looked down affectionately into the tender grey eyes that had
barely left his face since he entered the
room—"this is our very last evening together. To-night I must give you up to
your husband, and you and I shall never
be all in all to one another again! Do you
hear me, Lu? You and I must part, so to
speak, in another short hour for ever!
Why, you laugh, girl! Has this parting,
then, no sorrow for you? Are you such a

wanton that it's only a change of lovers,
and a thing to smile at?" he asked, angrily,
pushing her hand impatiently away from
him, while his eyes darkened, and a heavy
cloud swept over his brow, making him
look like a fiend.   He loved the woman as
much as it was in his nature to love anything, although he would have sacrificed
her on the spot to better himself in the
smallest degree.

" Robert," she replied—and the joyous
laugh on her lips was hushed in a moment,
and replaced by a nervous and painful
quiver, as she felt his rude and repelling
gesture, and cowered beneath the anger in
his voice—" you must be mad! You and I
can never part in this world; for if anything robbed me of you, I swear I would
put an end to myself.   I *have* married a
gentleman; but why? to please you—to do

your bidding; for you know you wished it, that I might be able to help you. But, oh! I hate him!—*I hate him!*" she repeated, vehemently, hissing the words out from between her set teeth, " for he will have a right to the hours I might spend with you —to the love, that should only be yours, Robert, dear! But he can't part us entirely, any way. I shall still see you often, but not so often as now, perhaps," she sobbed, pressing his hand again and again to her lips, and leaning her ruddy head on his knee, whilst her tears coursed rapidly down her cheeks, and fell in big drops to the ground. And he, his rough heart melting at the sight of her genuine grief, stooped over her, and, raising her up, soothed her as gently as lay in his power.

" Robert," she resumed after a little,

when he had wiped her tears away, and
peace was restored between them, " promise me, when I go away from this, that
nothing shall make you forget me! Swear
it, or my heart will break. Swear that no
other woman will ever take my place with
you!"

"I do swear it, Lucy," he said, as
emphatically as though he would not have
sworn his very ·soul away, without even a
scruple of conscience rebuking him for his
falsehood.   "You know, with all   my
faults, I am fond of you.   I wish now this
marriage had never taken place, for what
will be the good of money or anything,
without you !   But it can't be helped now,
and we must make the best on it. Come,
don't fret so, my girl," he whispered, kissing her, as she glanced up in his countenance with a mute gratitude for his kind

words, and with an implicit faith in his sincerity.

"Past nine already," she exclaimed, at length, "and he will be here soon. Only a few moments together now! Look, my dear!" And she put half a dozen bright sovereigns into his hand. "This will help to keep you comfortable, in case we don't meet for a few days."

And the shining sovereigns, that were the carefully hoarded-up store of the poor boy in Mandeville Terrace, who had denied himself every superfluity in life, barely allowing himself enough to keep body and soul together, in order to accumulate a small bridal offering for his wife, slipped quickly from her hand into Robert Minton's avaricious grasp, and from thence into his capacious pocket, to be squandered quickly away in the space of a few minutes in the intellectual games of " Aunt Sally" or skittles, in a neighbouring alley.

Suddenly there came a brisk pull at the door-bell, and David Welland, who had some few seconds before been decoyed away from his post of sentinel by the tempting fumes of the unusually attractive evening repast, rushed into the room, breathless and with his mouth full, articulating with considerable difficulty:

"Here he is, Lucy! Get along with you, quick," he added, hurriedly, to Minton, pushing that individual unceremoniously through the door on to the passage upon the kitchen-stairs. Then he hastened to answer the hasty summons, donning the most amiable expression he could muster up into his ugly physiognomy, to greet his well-born son-in-law.

The back slums of Islington had not yet arrived at the luxury—if luxury it can be called to have the tympanum of the human ear endangered some dozen times in a dozen hours—of " knockers."

Bells were the prevailing fashion in the locality, and the sole method of communication with the inmates of the dwellings open to the visitor, no matter whether he were a " nob" or the dustman.

This time it was the " harbinger of woe," the postman, who had given the impetuous twang at the wire, probably in sheer irritation at being deprived of his especial prerogative, the peremptory " rat-tat;" and David Welland, on reclosing the door, carried the missive that had been delivered to the light, and wonderingly scrutinized its exterior.

A large square envelope, sealed with a monogram, "M.L.," and addressed to

"Miss Welland,

6, Bridge Street,

Islington,"

in a man's hand that had evidently trembled, judging from the zigzag formation of the letters. The outside did not disclose much, and curiosity, worse than any woman's, strongly impelled him to peep into the interior, but a wholesome awe of his imperious daughter got the mastery over him, and restrained his fingers from tampering more freely with what did not belong to him, so he took it into the parlour and gave it to its rightful owner.

Meanwhile, Lucy had been briskly employed in putting the unsavoury *débris* of the evening repast carefully out of sight, and having arranged the room, and smoothed the braids of hair that had been somewhat ruffled by the contact of Robert Minton's coat-sleeve, she sat awaiting the advent of the new-comer in the most lady-like *pose* she could assume, with a piece of flimsy needlework lying in her lap.

In spite of all her vehement asseverations of " hatred," she was, womanlike, averse to appearing aught but enchanting in the eyes of the man whom she knew admired her.

Jumping off her seat, she snatched the letter, tore it open, and hastily conned the contents.

" Lucy, I know all !

" How I have been deceived, betrayed, outraged ! drawn into an act of folly, or rather madness, which has ruined me for ever! Oh! had you no pity, no spark of compunction for him who both loved and trusted you? pretending to render back his affection sevenfold, whilst you belonged, body and soul, to another! And *such* another! Great Heavens! when I think of my rival, my blood boils, and there is *no* vengeance, that I could not willingly take upon *him*. But *you*, Lucy, I do not hate; nay, I even love you still! But reason is stronger than passion within me now, and I never wish to look upon your fair, false face again.

"You and I shall never meet upon earth—do you understand? But still we are man and wife, and the miserable chain that binds us—though extended to its fullest length, though chafing and galling to both—will yet only be severed by death.

" You have entailed upon me a lonely future—a loveless, solitary existence; and blasted every hope of happiness I had in the world; and yet whilst you live, I have sworn before the God, who looked down upon our marriage vows, that no other woman shall fill the place by my side that *should* have been yours for ever and ever. You have rendered my life 'cold, and dark, and dreary,' and still I have no curse in my heart to give you.

" Only an earnest prayer, that time may bring you repentance for your deadly sin towards me, and gain you as full a pardon from the Heaven, your falsity mocked, as you now have from your husband.— M. L."

" Foiled! father," she cried, passionately, with her cheeks all on flame with anger,

and her eyes flashing wildly. " It's all up :
he has found out everything, somehow, and
we shall never see him again !"

" But you are his wife: he can't *help*
seeing you," the old man whimpered out,
peevishly. Was this the end of all their
plotting and scheming, he thought, to be
foiled at last by a mere stripling, a beardless
boy? Were all his grand visions of a comfortable old age going to melt into thin air
like this—the tower of hope that he had
built upon the foundation of his daughter's
elevation into a higher sphere? Was he
doomed still to labour on and on for the
remainder of his days, by the sweat of his
brow, for a livelihood, after all his antici-
pations of what the play calls the " Nigger's
Paradise," the luxury of keeping his hat on
his head, and his hands in his pockets,
alias idleness? His amount of book learn-

ing had not told him that idleness
is the Dead Sea, swallowing up all
virtue—the self-made sepulchre of a living
man !

" We *must* find him, Lucy, and we'll
have the law against him—the law of our
noble land, that is always so just and good;
and if we can't have *him*, we'll have
damages for desertion. *Heavy* damages,
eh, Lucy ?"

And his eyes twinkled greedily at
the very notion of the *L. S. D.* the
court would adjudge to the poor deserted
wife.

" Yes, that's all very well," she replied;
"but where can you find him? London
is a very large place, father, and we have
no clue to him, excepting his name, and that
may be a false one. But, no: it's on his
seal. We will advertise for him, and it we

are foiled after all this bother, it will be a
nuisance, for there's my dress and all the
rest of the wedding things unpaid for!
Robert!" she called out, and notwithstanding the failure of her scheme for worldly
aggrandizement and wealth—in spite of a
natural feminine feeling of anger and mortification at being "left," there was a sort
of ringing gladness in her loud accents.

"Robert, come in! Don't be afraid.
No husband, after all! only a trumpery
letter. Read it!" and she looked over
his shoulder while he perused the
document.

When he had finished reading it,
she never glanced at the expression of
his face, but throwing herself into his
arms, said, "And now I am yours, dear;
yours only, for ever!"

"So *this* game's up, and no more bleeding likely of that white-faced stripling. Curse him !" was what passed through Robert Minton's mind, as he bit his lip hard, and affectionately returned Lucy's embrace.

CHAPTER I.

TWO HEARTS.

" By Castor!   Love
    Hath both its gall and honey in abundance,
    Sweet to the taste; but in it we swallow bitter,
    Even till we loathe !"

" No sooner met, than they looked; no sooner looked,
than they loved! no sooner loved, than they sighed !"
Shakespeare.

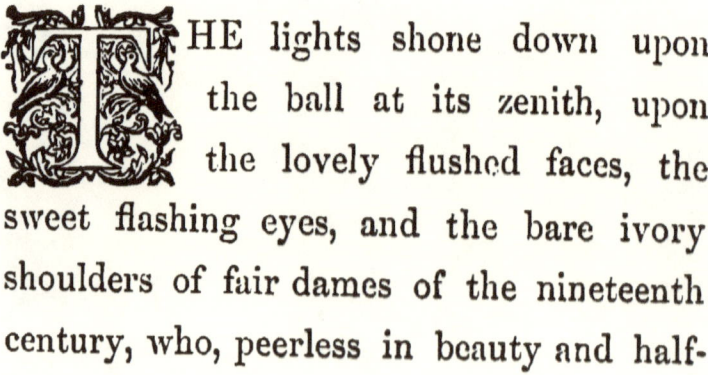HE lights shone down upon
the ball at its zenith, upon
the lovely flushed faces, the
sweet flashing eyes, and the bare ivory
shoulders of fair dames of the nineteenth
century, who, peerless in beauty and half-

draped in form, floated gracefully in aerial garments through the quadrille, or were whirled round in voluptuous evolutions, as Byron aptly has it—

" With hands promiscuously applied
Round the slight waist or down the glowing side."

Through the heated temperature of the crowded room stole the fragrance of perfumed ambrosial curls and ebon braids, mingling with the scent of exquisite exotics, whose shining leaves and gorgeous colouring contrasted beautifully with the alabaster tints of the bosoms against which they closely nestled.

A scene of revelry, roses, and loveliness; upon which two or three men looked, as they lounged together indolently near the entrance of the ball-room.

The man with the Norman type of physiognomy and drooping tawny mous-

tache was Arthur Gordon, a young Scotch
Baronet, owning a lengthy pedigree that
dated from the time that "Wallace bled."
He was rich in an amplitude of the choicest
things that can be bestowed on the sons of
earth—youth, health, and wealth, good
looks, inexhaustible spirits, and a bijou of
an estate, romantically situated in the heart
of the bonnie Highlands — a mansion
perched on a lovely hill that, bathed in
sunshine or lying in depths of cool shadow,
towered high towards the blue sky—with
its sides lined by luxuriant wilds of gorse
and yellow broom, whilst around rose a
fulness of green, and miles upon miles of
purple feathery heather, intersected by
crystal streams, running like so many silvery threads through the flowery pastures.

Very different in pecuniary position to
the owner of " Silvernest" was Maurice

Lynn, an *homme de lettres*, and far from affluent, although possessing a sufficiency for moderate wants.

His character also was a direct opposition to that of his companion, for he was staid, serious, and slightly cynical—traits that were antipodean *au dernier dégré* to Gordon's laughter-loving versatile temperament, and yet curiously enough, as though in exemplification of the proverb, *les extrèmes se touchent*, the two were the firmest of allies, and, if possible, inseparable.

"Maurice!" said Gordon, suddenly, after a prolonged silence, during which he had been watching covertly, with an amused expression on his features, the stolid indifference, amounting to apathy, with which Lynn surveyed each bright creature who flitted to and fro before them, his gaze never lingering two consecutive moments

on any one particular belle, but following
the movements of each in succession, with
a strange sort of dreamy *nonchalance* in
his eyes.

"Do you know, I often wonder, old
fellow, if there exists upon earth *any*
woman possessing sufficient attractions to
enchain your fancy even for a short while!
The Man in the Iron Mask could scarcely
have presented a more imperturbable exterior than your face has worn during the
last half hour, whilst your eyes have been
regaled on a perfect garden of rich and
glowing delights—flowers of all sorts, full-
blown and budding!"

"'Pon my soul! I do believe Helen herself would have failed in arresting your
regard, and that a search for a woman to
your fastidious liking would be as long and
as futile as Diogenes' hunt after honesty.

And yet beauty is a grand thing! Isn't it Keats who says, 'A thing of beauty is a joy for ever?'"

"Was it Keats? I can't recollect just now. Madame Rachel, I should fancy, probably," Lynn replied, indifferently; but a shade stole over his countenance as he added—

"But the fact is that I seem to care for nothing! If this ball-room were transformed into a seraglio, and my humble self into Abdul Aziz, and I had *congé d'élire* any one of the smiling houris before me, I swear I should be nonplussed. Either beauty has lost its influence over me completely, or else the only type of it that could, perhaps, 'fetch' me ever so slightly, never appears. The long and the short of the matter is, that I am 'used up,' literally blasé to extinction. I have

either made a very bad use of life, or else life
has ill used me shamefully.   I only know
that I arrived long ago at the conclusion
that I am not capable of 'falling in love,'
as it is called.   The naked boy spreads his
meshes for me in vain, and yet I am not
such an idiot as to fancy myself a miso-
gynist.   But, somehow, pretty faces and I
seem to have nothing in common with one
another.   Every charm that enthrals other
men passes me by, scarcely touching me so
much as the stroke of a feather, and leaving behind no deeper impress than the
breath of the soft summer wind.   There
is always a wretched hiatus in either my
heart or imagination that nothing can fill
up!"

"Humbug! *mon cher :* no hiatus, only a
bad digestion, or else the grumblings of a
mind unhealthily morbid.   You think that

love has lost all potency for you, just because you may have been victimized by
Cupid once in your life, and deceived. It
would, indeed, be very hard lines if, just
because you mistook in boyish folly, the
paltry glimmer of a 'farthing dip' for a
'real ray of light from Allah,' as Byron
calls it."

"Yes, but not in earnest, only in
poetry," interrupted Lynn. "Those little
animals that existed on the river Hypanis
were typical of *his* loves, living only twelve
hours, dying in youth and loveliness at
eight o'clock in the morning, but reaching
a miserable state of decrepitude, if their existence was prolonged any longer. You
have quoted unhappily, Arthur!"

"A little learning is a dangerous thing,"
by Jove, and only makes your brain sick.
To be of a philosophical nature is good

sometimes, for philosophy enables one to bear things serenely; but I would rather eschew it and accept the usual compound of sweet and acidity. Perpetual sunshine would irritate the eye, and even the nectar of the Gods would soon become horribly cloying. Life and love to me should be symbolized by a repast of *pâtés*, piquante with Cayenne and spicy condiments, washed down by a draught of sparkling Clicquot, and wound up by a sweet and luscious peach. There are lots of fellows who go in for starvation of feeling and mortification of the flesh, on principle, but the result is often contrary to what they expect, for eventually they become worse than caged beasts, doubly rapacious, from restriction in food and isolation from their kind. Ergo, those hypocritical monks. I wager that a regular man about town hasn't half the unbridled flights of passion that seize *them*, in spite of all their abstinence from pleasure and dinners of lentils."

"In fact, 'Life's Goblet' you would freely press, and wish it 'hot, sweet, and strong,' like the peg of an ancient crone after a hard day's charing; but remember what the old Dominie used to say at school, when a warm joint one day portended cold scraps the next:—

'Festo die si quid prodigeris,
Profecto egere liceat nisi peperceris'—

and be prepared for the trying contrast!"

"But Lynn," said Reggy Peel, a smart, sharp-witted young fellow in the Foreign Office, "why on earth should you take as jaundiced a view of existence, as if you were as elderly as Methuselah, or as acid as a lemon, or eschew woman and society like

a misanthrope ?   Those men are only made
to be unsociable 'who like nobody, are like
nobody, and are liked by nobody.'   All
women are not the Scylla and Charybdis
of human life.   Wait a bit till the right
one turns up to *bouleverser* all your
notions.   Why even a single glance might
melt the pillar of ice into Vesuvian lava,
— and transmogrify the stoic into a
spoon !"

"Not if I know it!   *Omnia vanitas !*
There's a picture illustrative of that fact
for which I have a weakness.   Have you
seen it?   'A nude female figure, gleaming
up through sunlight from a snowy couch,
testifying pleasure,' with all sorts of
emblems of the nothingness of everything
surrounding it."

"I am as insensible to profiles cut like
cameos as I am to the laughing face of

a Hebe. The blue-black tresses of an Eastern sultana, or the locks of gold adorning the purest blonde—the willowy limbs of a Juno, or the voluptuous form of a Venus—are alike impotent to touch me; and as to the '*beaux yeux*' of the sex, their looks fall as harmlessly as though I were a second Bartimeus. No feminine proximity makes my heart give one throb the quicker; no rustle of a petticoat accelerates the blood in my veins. But the worst of it all is, that I don't know whether such a state of *statu-quo* existence is a matter of congratulation or not."

"Of course not," exclaimed Gordon. "One might as well be a pulse plant, half human, half vegetable. Life isn't worth having at any price, if every feeling, love included, appears tame and uninteresting.

Even to have cared for some one once, is something to look back upon with pleasure."

" Rather a lugubrious one when the verb *amore* is conjugated in the past tense, surely."

" Not a bit of it. It's a sort of oasis in the desert. The recollection of the pleasant little episode lingers, and gives a halo of romance to the prosaic worldly feelings that come later in life. Besides, a man must be all the better for having at any one period loved, and been loved by a really good and pure woman, and like—

   ' The stained web that whitens in the sun,
      Grows pure by being purely shone upon.' "

" *Bravissimo*, Arthur! you speak like a book!" laughed Reggy.

" No—

    ' My only books
    Were women's looks.' "

"And a prodigious quantity of deceit you must have learnt, then," asserted Maurice.

"But surely *you* have never felt the fierce, passionate love, or the patient, all-enduring affection, that leaves indelible traces behind? You, the *papillon*, full of fun and *persiflage*, but never showing on your wings a sign of having been singed!"

"I wish I was a butterfly, &c., for it must be the jolliest thing in the world—roving from flower to flower, gathering honey wherever you can; never lingering long enough on one blossom to reach satiety, but finding zest and enjoyment in charming variety. ' Love endures no tie,' and *perjuria ridet amantium Jupiter*. A *quid pro quo*, Lynn, for your school Latin. Who will gainsay the fact that

Phiz and flirtation are nice enough things?"

" One *must* be easily satisfied if they suffice for niceness. One might as well go in for an Oriental heaven: all black eyes and sherbet."

" *Vive la bagatelle!* say I; and as for you, ' a grand passion' is probably *in petto,* if it were only a vengeance from the rosy urchin for scouting at him. By Jove!"

And Gordon stopped short, seizing Lynn's arm, and whispered, *sotto voce,* in an agitated tone, that was strangely dissimilar to the bantering voice he had been speaking in—

" Who would have dreamt of seeing *her* here!"

" Who?"

" Lettice Grey, the only girl I ever

loved, or ever shall love, and who has it in her power to make me happy or miserable all my life!"

"Arthur, old boy, you are contradiction itself! A minute ago you were advocating inconstancy, and now, like a moonstruck lover, here you are in tragic rhapsody worse than Romeo's, apostrophizing some Nemesis who has suddenly risen up to rebuke you for your Lotharian discourse. Where is the avenging goddess?"

"There! Could any one divine that within such a form, there beat a heart full of falsity! I am not particularly vindictive by nature; but, hang it! I swear I could find a wish to see her pride crushed, as I stand here and see all the smiles she is bestowing on those cursed puppets obsequiously dancing attendance upon her,

while she seems to delight in the adulation
she receives. She sees *me*, too, and re-
doubles her gaiety.   Oh, woman! they
may call you a ' ministering angel,' but
you are a far greater source of torment
than of joy."

"Calm yourself," said Lynn, soothingly.
He saw that Gordon was really in earnest,
and he had the good taste to abstain from
any misplaced " chaffing" or expression of
the surprise he felt, in seeing the lively
Baronet turned all at once into a lovesick
and despairing swain.

"Arthur, you are probably doing her
injustice, and later you may blame yourself
for allowing doubts of her to enter your
mind. If she *does* see you, and laughs, and
appears engrossed by others, why, what
then? It is only a fact, from which a
flattering or unflattering deduction can be

drawn, according to your own will. Don't let the green-eyed monster run away with you, and warp your judgment. No one can guess from an exterior that is extorted by the *convenances* the real feelings that exist beneath a surface of sparkling smiles. God knows! how often I have carried a very heavy heart into a festive scene, where perhaps my laugh may have sounded the loudest, and even the most genuine in the room. We do not require to live very long to find out that *les apparences sont trompeuses;* and many a time a poor woman may be suffering torture in her soul, and yet she may possess sufficient commendable pride not to 'wear her heart upon her sleeve, for daws to peck at.' But which of the three Graces, you pointed towards, is *the* one? That magnificent girl with the

imperial brow and eyes like twin stars,
or the pretty plump little woman by her
side?"

"Neither. The tall girl is Miss Chesterton; the lady next to her is a stranger
to me."

"Don't you know who *she* is?
Then *I* will tell you," Reggy Peel re-
joined. "She is Mrs. Marmaduke Smith,
née Janet Morton, the Irish beauty that all
London went mad about when she made
her *début*. Two years ago *I* was her
accepted suitor, but the diplomatic horizon
looking shady, and no likelihood of an
appointment turning up, Miss Janet bowled
me over, *sans ceremonie*, for the rich stockbroker. I never felt so small and so
ashamed of my ancestry as when I got cir-
cumvented by a 'Smith.' Faugh! a con-
venient enough cognomen, however, for

who would be insane enough to plunge
into the intricacies of a ' Smith's' genealogy
so long as he was nicely rolled up in crisp
bank-notes.   Money! Leviathan power—
Juggernauth monster, that crushes beneath
its wheels every other recommendation a
man may possess.   Hang titles, and talents
too, unless it be the talent of turning all
you touch into good hard cash!   Even a
hideous old buffer of seventy, coming in
for half a million, can afford to give himself
airs.   He is no longer old—he is no longer
ugly; he has only got to show himself to
be courted and admired.   Only to hold out
his withered hands, and the prettiest, loveliest lips will gladly kiss them.   Only to
display his bank-book, and the most youthful belle of Belgravia will be his.   He has
only to command, and all women will be
his slaves.   It is for such as him, a super-

annuated Monte Cristo, that the purest
and the vilest of the sex were evidently
made; and he has only to drop his snuff-
stained handkerchief amongst them, and
it will be disputed for and as eagerly
claimed, as the golden apple of Paris! Mrs.
Smith's ambition now is to be considered
a literary character, and she cannot exist
out of an atmosphere of savants! Those
two men hanging over her are fashionable
scribblers; and one of them, Terence, goes
in for *homme galant* as well. The other is
in the gum-and-stamp office; and both
are 'lions' who find plenty of 'Unas'
in London society to pet and spoil
them."

"Then the fair girl is your especial
weakness, Arthur?"

"Yes; and I have looked into those
great innocent blue eyes of hers until

they seemed to hold out to me the proof a heaven whose azure they rival.
I told her frankly that she had become
everything in the world to me; and she
put her hand into mine, and hid her
face on my shoulder, and swore to
be my wife! But what's the wisdom of
retrospection! it only makes a fellow feel
doubly down."

"Yes, but, you know, 'confession is
good,' etcetera; and I am interested in
this little romance of your life, which you
have contrived to keep so dark."

"Well, to cut a long story short, there
were no obstacles to surmount: everything
went smoothly as a marriage-bell. We
were as happy as a couple of children.
Suddenly a cloud arose—a paltry speck,
rather—jealousy, misunderstanding, and
so on, increased it into a thunder-bolt

at last; then *that* burst, and left me wretched."

" And took you off to Venice for six months, to try the cure of Venetian tresses. I remember you left England with an unusually crestfallen countenance."

" Yes; but *she* did not suffer, and is as smiling and serene as ever, as though nought had occurred to ruffle the even tenor of *her* life. I have never set eyes upon her till to-night."

" Here's some balm for you. I am a bit of a physiognomist, and I see no coldness or falsity in the glances that she turns covertly, but very frequently, this way. Make it up with her if you really love her, Arthur, and you will find it was only a ' cloud with a silver lining,' after all, that came between you."

" No offence to your taste, old fellow,

car il n'y a pas de règle sans exception; but I, as a rule, *hate* fair women. They are generally as treacherous as panthers, and often as vicious. The other girl is more my type of beauty, but ten chances to one she is either stupid or wicked."

"Maurice, your eternal cynicism grates upon me, in spite of my irritated feelings. You expect a *rara avis* instead of a woman. However, you had better be introduced to her, and I almost hope she will revenge her whole sex by breaking your heart—that is, if there is such an absurdity as a broken heart, or *suivant* your hypothesis, hearts of any kind."

"Who is she?"

"Daughter of Sir John Chesterton, a pompous, fussy old Baronet, emulated in stiff-neckedness by the haughty dame, his wife. The family dates from near the Deluge, *ou un peu près*, and have extensive estates in Lincolnshire, besides a palatial mansion in Eaton Square. Violet Chesterton is an only child, and an heiress, and, *par conséquence*, a natural target for matrimonial shafts of all sorts. *On dit*, that she, too, has a leaven of the family pride, and that she is ridiculously quixotic in her defence of an immaculateness that nineteenth - century men don't often come up to. No one has hitherto appeared to reach up to her impossible standard, and she never condescends to flirting like other girls. Now *you*, Maurice, cannot be classed as a fortune-hunter, and you may succeed in pleasing her as a pleasant acquaintance. Friendship with a pretty woman is agreeable enough, although I confess I have not much faith myself in its existence between the sexes."

"La Fontaine said that love is but a shadow of the morning, that decreases as day advances; but that friendship is the shadow of the evening, that lengthens with the setting sun."

"La Fontaine must have been a block of ice, like yourself," laughed Reggy Peel.

"Platonics are awfully jolly things, I dare say, provided you have moral courage to stick to them. They don't entail on you a tenter - hook sort of existence, with a continual sword of Damocles suspended by a hair over your head; they don't feed you on a diet of 'honey and bitter aloes,' with the bitter predominating considerably;

and they don't give you half the bother
and pain of being a miserable shuttle-
cock, wafted hither and thither, north,
south, east, and west—by Cupid's capricious battledore!"

*   *   *   *

" May I introduce my friend Mr.
Lynn?" Gordon said, later in the evening; and by the time the lady had
bowed her acknowledgment of the introduction, Arthur had quietly lounged
away, and Violet Chesterton, lifting up
her eyes, looked straight into a face
that exactly realized her ideal.

CHAPTER II.

OMNIA VINCIT AMOR.

"Love is a sweet idolatry, enslaving all the soul,
A mighty spiritual force, warring with the dullness
    of matter—
An angel mind breathed into a mortal !
    *   *   *   *   *   *
Love ! what a volume in a word, an ocean in a tear,
A seventh heaven in a glance, a whirlwind in a sigh,
The lightning in a touch, a Millennium in a moment !"
                              Proverbial Philosophy.

"To love, and at the same time to be wise, is
scarcely granted even to a god."

N undoubted *homme du monde*,
Maurice Lynn's character was
yet somewhat inconsistent, if
looked upon in the hackneyed acceptance

of that term.   He was excessively shrewd
and far-seeing, but the power of penetra-
tion which unveiled to him in all their
meanness and deformity, the vices of the
human mind, had failed to render him
either particularly cautious or calculating
in the acquaintance he formed.   He was
true in judgment, although as impulsive in
his real temperament as an infant, but he
contrived to disguise his naturally strong
feelings under a mountain of seeming
ice.

Sceptical of genuine goodness in both
sexes, he was yet wonderfully ardent in his
implicit and unwavering faith in the few
he really liked and respected.   An accom-
plished scholar, a profound thinker, and an
occasional dreamer, he was a man who
lived to some purpose.

Unlike the majority of men with whom

he was in daily association, his life had been far from a frivolous one, and untoward circumstances had shown him a good deal more of the shady side of existence with its innumerable knocks and brunts, than of the summer portion of it, that is filled with poetry and spread with roses. Many a "crumpled leaf" had, however, strewed his path.

Nine years ago he had been a clerk, and almost a drudge, in a great banking firm in the City—a berth procured for him with infinite difficulty by an old and influential friend of his family; but, nevertheless, a berth that yielded in return for ten wearisome hours of diurnal labour the magnificent remuneration of an annual stipend of some sixty pounds.

Still, during the lifetime of the only parent that was left to him, he had plodded

and worked on, patiently and uncomplainingly, at the uninteresting study of ledgers;
and had allowed himself neither time, nor
licence of imagination for soaring into
higher branches of literature, or dwelling
on a less prosaic aspect of life than that
which was open to him within the circum-
scribed space contained between the four
walls of the banker's office. When at
length he found himself alone in the world,
with no relative dependent on his daily
exertions, he gladly threw up the irksome
stuffy berth, and with the very few
hundreds that formed the whole of his
patrimony he commenced a new career in
the Great Babylon—the most uncertain
career he could possibly have chalked out
for himself, viz., an author's.

It was in sad, sober, and earnest truth,
a very tempestuous ocean on which he had

been courageous enough to risk his "little all," with no finish, apparently, to the rocks and shoals that were to be encountered in the passage, and with no end of violent buffetings with the overwhelming and nearly submerging waves of criticism that was occasionally not only ill-natured, but positively unjust, until the critics and reviewers of the nineteenth century became the very bugbears of his life, and over and over again he inwardly endorsed the sentiment that had emanated from the breast of a "forlorn and shipwrecked brother." The fangs of a bear, the tusks of a wild boar, do not bite worse and make deeper gashes than a goosequill sometimes! No, even the badger himself, who is said to be so tenacious of his bite that he will not give over his hold until his teeth meet!

8—2

Aristotle, when asked by what criterion we should judge of the merits of a book, replied, "When an author has said every-thing that he ought, nothing but what he ought, and says that as he ought."

The critics of the day were as exacting and severe as the Grecian philosopher.

"Let there be '*gall enough*' in thy ink, though thou write with a goose-pen, no matter !" was an exordium to their heart's content; so instead of occasionally handling with gentleness, or even now and then amiably overlooking some of the blemishes that met their view, thereby bestowing a little encouragement on him who wrote with the earnest desire, if failing in the power, to merit approval, they seemed to revel with a malicious joy in gushes of censoriousness, piti-lessly mutilating each carefully-penned

sentence, until it came disgracefully limp-
ing out into the world, and crushing
each flight of imagination until it lay a
hideous commonplace, bereft of all that
could make it sound even readable to
the public.

Poor Maurice would often catch himself
poring sadly and hopelessly over the pages
of a review that mercilessly and ruthlessly
slashed away at some particularly pet
passage over which he had spent hours of
thought, and would feel inclined to ejacu-
late, bitterly enough—

> " Satire or sense, alas! can Sporus feel,
> Who breaks a butterfly upon a wheel!"

From early youth he had been imbued
with melancholy and somewhat morbid
views of life—that " the world had nothing
solid, nothing desirable in it; that it was
only a fashion, and a fashion that passeth

away; that the tenderest affections end; that honours are but specious titles that time effaces; that pleasures are only amusements that have a lasting and painful repentance; that riches escape by their own instability; that grandeur is but mouldering, and that glory and reputation lose themselves in the abyss of eternal oblivion; —that, in fact, thus rolls the torrent of the world whatever pains are taken to stop it, and that everything is carried away by a rapid train of passing events," were disheartening truths for a stripling to study; but, nevertheless, he preferred them to the light sensational romances that have generally so great a charm for youth.

He struggled on manfully, however, in spite of the discouraging barriers that rose up continually in his path; and although he did not exactly " wake up one morning to find himself famous," yet success came to him at length by *soupçons*, to reward him for his sturdy and unceasing efforts.

And when he had succeeded in securing a competency that precluded a necessity for turning his brains to account, he yet scribbled on from sheer love and taste for literature, whom he had constituted his sole mistress, and at whose shrine he was not only a willing slave but even an enthusiastic devotee.

He was twenty-eight years old now, and nine years of that period he had led a studious and sedentary life, rarely going in for more than bare glimpses of the world, and eschewing as much as lay in his power the myth, alluring but dangerous, that that world calls "pleasure."

He believed firmly that a determined

votary of pleasure was one " who desires to be happier than any man *can* be, and is less happy than most men *are*— one, in fact, who seeks happiness every-where but where it is to be found, and who out-toils the labourer not only without his wages, but even paying dearly for it."

The slave of pleasure, it is said, sinks into a kind of voluptuous dotage; intoxicated with present delights, and care-less of everything else, his days and nights glide away in luxury and vice, and he has no care but one, and that is to keep thought away. But how like an opium-eater's dream such an existence must be, with occasional fits of wakefulness, in the short space of which as much pain must be endured as would more than counterbalance the pleasure of whole ages of blissful trances!

Long, long ago, a few hours of his life, had done Maurice right good service, although they had made him suffer bitterly at the time. They had induced him to "sow his wild oats" at a far earlier period of manhood than is usually the case.

Women and pleasure had become to him dark shadows of the past, to be dreaded and shunned in the future, instead of appearing to be sources of enjoyment in the present; but with unbelief in the feminine sex came a certain quantum of cynicism that in the eyes of many marred his character. His studious ways had imparted a peculiar gravity to his manner, which is rare in an age in which men, counting their years by threescore and ten, affect the

buoyant spirits and frisky juvenility of
boyhood; but there was a species of
" attrait" in the very fits of abstraction
that crept over him at times, asserting
their ascendancy even amidst society, and
drawing him away, as it seemed, from
the outer world into a world of his
own—a world that was evidently peopled
with melancholy fancies, judging by the
tinge of sadness that those reveries always
left upon his visage.

His personal advantages were great.

Hanging up, in an out-of-the-way
corner of a picture gallery at Dresden,
is a small cabinet painting, resembling
an old Velasquez, and labelled "Saint
Augustin." A rich but very dark back-
ground, showing up a face in startling
relief, as though it were chiselled in
marble.

The eyes deep-set and large, with a sort of "far-off" look in them, under a pair of well-defined brows.

The whole countenance superb like a Greek god's, but lacking warmth and mobility in the rigidness of the lines round the mouth, and the severe regularity of each delicate feature.

Maurice might have sat as the original of the saint's portrait, except that when he smiled, which was but rarely, all the coldness faded right out of his face, and an expression of unutterable softness stole over his lips.

He was a tall man with a lithe figure, possessing far more of elegance in it, than muscular strength, and his intellectual countenance was pale with nightly vigils.

"A slave of the lamp," he paid the

penalty of his badge, by a loss of the fresh
colouring, that never goes hand in hand
with a consumption of " midnight oil," but
which constitutes with many people manly
beauty and vigour. With others, though
they might have been in the minority, his
principal charm was the very refinement of
the *spirituelle* face.

He had a free independence about him,
and a thorough indifference to general
popularity. To those whom he desired to
please, his voice and manner were fascina-
ting in the extreme. And in a woman who
possessed sufficient capability and taste to
appreciate properly the " nobility" of his
type of physiognomy, he was just the
being to excite profound admiration and
devotion, and to be placed upon a pedestal
of perfection for her to fall down and
worship. When he conversed with one of

the opposite sex, which was not very frequently, there was, in spite of his avowed scepticism in feminine worth, a deference in his tone which insensibly flattered and pleased the fair creature he addressed, and his eyes, ordinarily wearing a cold reflective expression, acquired potent attraction for any woman who fancied herself gifted with the power of drawing a warmer look into them when they turned upon her.

Only a few weeks had elapsed since the memorable ball at which Violet Chesterton had met her " Fate," as she inwardly called him, and she had learnt the great lesson of life by heart. The verb *amo*, with regard to Maurice, had been conjugated by her already fifty times a day in every tense and mood—" practice makes perfect"—and she was as proficient in her task as though she had been studying it for years instead of days. She would watch for a flood of " love-light" to well up into those serious hazel eyes, and when it came a strange rapture would fill her bosom. She had turned over a new leaf in existence, and the perusal of it imparted a zest and colouring to life that was blissful beyond expression. She utterly forgot her real age, and dated the first hour of her being from that moment when she had first looked upon him.

And where in all the world could have been found a more invincible proof of *omnia vincit amor* than in Maurice? Maurice, the unbeliever, the sceptic, the cynical ridiculer of all earthly affection!

It was love, passion, madness, or all three combined, that had hurled away to the four winds of heaven, in a brief moment, all his cherished sentiments, all his beloved philosophy of many a long year! But how could he have looked at her and doubted that goodness and truth really existed in this world? How could he have spoken to her, and believed that such lips as hers could frame aught savouring of falsity or deceit? How could he have touched her and not acknowledged within himself that, in spite of all he had so lately avowed, he was still capable of loving, that his heart was not only *not* " dead," but possessed the human attributes of worshipping, rejoicing, and suffering!

She was the "ray of light" of which Gordon had spoken; but why had cruel fate cast her into his path, when her presence for a little while could but

make the darkness in which destiny
had placed him, still more terribly
visible?

Since the two had met, circumstances
had thrown them, *nolens volens*, continually together. Maurice had, day by day,
emerged more and more out of his shell,
and had become an altered man. He
seemed to have thrown off all his ordinary reserve and apathy, and went
into society with a light buoyancy of
spirit, which, if not reaching quite to the
noisy hilarity of some men, yet presented
a remarkable contrast to his former de-
meanour.

Arthur Gordon looked on amazed at
the sudden transformation; but Gordon
was entirely without "guile," and was
one of those open, unsuspecting creatures
that never think of *diving* for motives,

accepting willingly the surface so long as it be a pleasant one. What on earth mattered it to him, to trouble himself by questioning as to *cause*, when the *effect* was agreeable? Maurice had grown infinitely jollier, and consequently was a better companion than ever.

Moreover, he had enough work on his hands on his own account, and all his time was employed in reflecting as seriously as any Commander-in-Chief, over the wisest manœuvres for the siege of a citadel that appeared impervious to any method of attack.

A wilful capricious fairy, with the loveliest mignonne figure in the world, and an innocent Hebe face, Miss Lettice Grey, once more having turned up on the tapis, had resumed her despotic reign in the Baronet's honest heart; but he had not as yet ventured to hold up before those laughing turquoise eyes the flag of truce, for she was so cruel to him, playing fast and loose with his feelings, just as her variable mood dictated. Now and then a kinder look, a furtive smile, would almost bring him, a humble suppliant at her side; then a flirty move-ment, a coquettish arch glance shot else-where, would arrest his flying steps, and leave him bitterly riled, and angrily venting his annoyance on the unoffend-ing hirsute glory that adorned his upper lip, and of which many men were envious. Arrived at years of discretion, and pos-sessing a moderate amount of brains, he yet lacked the wisdom to know

"Where is the man who has the power and skill
To stem the torrent of a woman's will?
For if she will, *she will*, you may depend on't,
And if she wont, *she wont*, and there's an end on't !"

The provincial town in which both Maurice Lynn and the Chestertons were temporary visitors, presented but a limited society, the members of which naturally frequented the same places of resort and amusement, the same balls, fêtes, and pic-nics, each of which afforded easy facilities for furthering a desirable acquaintance.

Thus a morning scarcely dawned upon the lovers—for lovers they had speedily become — without the blessed assurance of a meeting, somewhere or somehow, before the breaking of another day.

But though these looked-for meetings were of daily occurrence, Maurice, though he had perhaps *implied* love, had never by word *avowed* it.

His looks and his manner testified openly enough to the feelings which the girl had awakened in him; but never had he embodied his sentiments in a single sentence; never, in spite of many a favourable opportunity, in spite of the very encouragement that he could scarcely fail to read in Violet's sweet eyes, those speaking eyes, that he had likened to twin stars, and which had become in truth the only beacons he knew, had he dared to breathe his passion, or to seek for an acknowledgment of reciprocity from the lips that sometimes seemed almost to *woo* him to come nearer them.

But though wearing a gay and lively exterior abroad, alone, and at home, the old fits of gloom began to reassume their sway over him, and none but himself knew the extent of the fearful struggle within him, or guessed how terribly hard it had already become for him, to resist the mute, but eloquent pleading of those dear lips and eyes, and to stifle back the passionate words that burnt in his breast for utterance.

Conscience — and with him conscience had hitherto been powerful enough—now continually persuaded him to be strong, and to flee from temptation; but for the first time in his life he tried to chase away the "still small voice," feeling that it was impossible for him to break through the spell that bound him to Violet's side, even though love threatened to conquer, when both honour and principle bade him be dumb.

It was brought home to him now how utterly moral cowardice and a guilty heart go hand in hand.

If he could but be brave, and obey the impulse to do rightly, saying

"No" decidedly to himself, and adhering to his sapient resolution—*but* he could not.

"But," it is said, is a more detestable combination of letters than any other. "No" is a surly, but honest fellow, speaks his mind rough and round at once; *but*, is only a sneaking, evasive, half-bred, exceptional sort of conjunction, and the man who uses it is lost.

Maurice soon persuaded himself that it would be just as futile a task to try and "enchain a wild buffalo with a garland of flowers," as to wrestle with the mightiness of the love that had become a portion of his being.

Violet, with eighteen years of experience, was not very *au fait* at the difficult reading of human nature, but she was old enough and intelligent enough to discover the existence of the tempest evidently warring within her lover's heart.

There were occasional moments when, torn by the conflicting emotions of anxiety and incertitude, absolute unhappiness prevailed over her, and she tormented herself by perplexing doubts and fears, and all the other unpleasant concomitants of "being in love," asking herself whether Maurice really cared for her or otherwise?

But such moments were very rare, and she felt at most times a happy and certain conviction, that though something deterred him from speaking, a true affection *did* exist and was her very own ; but what that fatal " something" was, remained to her an enigma long unsolved, and unexplained.

She could have staked her life on
his truth, and have vouched before all
the world, that he was no gay trifler,
like the many butterflies that fluttered
around her with honeyed speeches, and
specious flattery, meeting no kinder re-
sponse from her than their own in-
sincerity deserved.   He was assuredly
no fortune-hunter, dazzled into admiration and adulation, by the glitter of
her reputed wealth; no wanton wounder
of women's feelings, no male flirt, that
most despicable creature of the masculine species, searching for victims to
gratify his paltry vanity.   And there
was no apparent sensualism in his com-
position, prompting him to pursue for
awhile one who pleased his eye, but
who lacked the power to enchain his
footsteps, or to satisfy his erratic taste.

Violet, after the fashion of her sex, who, when Cupid has them under his thumb, are obstinately blind and deaf to any possible defects in the object of their affections, was convinced that Maurice was all that " her fancy painted him," and she would have answered as steadfastly for . him as for herself: so, weary of conjecturing, she resolved to bide her time patiently, and to leave the future to take care of itself. To her, her lover's daily presence was actual meat and drink and oxygen, leaving no desire ungratified, no wish unfulfilled. He was become the alpha and omega of everything— her all in all. She lived in a beatific dream from morn till night, and from night to morn; and so long as no prospect of parting from him came to

shadow her happy life, she was as blithe-
some as a bird.

But as day after day slipped by,
lengthening into weeks, and even months,
Sir John Chesterton and his lady-wife
grew less tolerant of the delay in the
open declaration of Maurice's sentiments, than the party most concerned
in the matter, was herself.

They could not naturally compre-
hend why a man, who was undoubtedly
Violet's very shadow, should be so
tardy in coming forward honourably, as
a claimant for her hand.

The Chestertons were proud old
people, and with the acute sensitive-
ness that always accompanies extreme
pride, they shrank painfully from having
their family matters made the theme
of babbling vulgar tongues at every

"cat - lap" that took place in the town.

Already meddling old maids and envious matrons of their own clique had made them perfectly *au courant* of the gossip, for there was no lack of *cancan* about, and the society, especially when demolition of reputation was the subject, might have been compared to a "heap of embers, which, when brought together in contact, burst into a flame, and devoured up everything."

The art of spreading scandal has been wisely likened to pin - making. There is usually some truth as foundation, according to the old French proverb—"*Il n'y a pas de fumée sans feu*," and that may represent the wire; this passes from hand to hand, whilst one gives it a polish, another a head, another a point, and so on.

Maurice Lynn was apparently in an eligible position to marry. Burke's "Landed Gentry" gave his family, and the social status they had held in Worcestershire, in full. He seemed to be his own master, and under these circumstances his behaviour rendered him a likely mark for virulent discussion. That there must be something *sub rosâ* to make him act as he was doing, was voted an undisputed fact; and with this suggestion administered to them homœopathically, in small but frequent doses, it was no wonder Sir John and his spouse grew distrustful of the man who seemed to be only a sort of "detrimental" after all—a mere stumbling-block in their daughter's path to forming a more brilliant alliance, and, in fact, accepting what to worldly folks is the *ne plus ultra* of terrestrial bliss, the coronet of a peeress,—for Violet had no paucity of offers, both from titled men and commoners.

Her fortune in itself, was a sufficient bait for needy noblemen seeking to re-suscitate their finances, had she been hideous as a Gorgon ; but wealth, united to a beauty, that in its radiance completely paled the loveliness of other women, made her a beautiful and golden prize, naturally desired by most who looked upon her.

Poor Maurice, in the midst of all his short-comings, was assuredly no " detrimental ;" he loved the girl too truly to be selfish, and he never attempted to monopolize her by word or deed, if a rival appeared

in the field; but would yield her up, without
a murmur, to any aspirant to her society,
although his cheek would grow pale as
death, as he watched her from his distant
corner, on another man's arm; and up in
his breast would rise an involuntary sigh,
smothered back by a valiant effort—a
sigh which though voiceless, never failed
in finding an echo in the heart of her
whom he had relinquished, accompanied
by a mutinous feeling at his unselfishness
in giving her up.

The diurnal meetings were brought to a
summary termination, by a sudden decision
of Sir John's to eschew parties for a while.
Invitations were steadily refused, and eyes
as curious as Argus's were kept on un-
happy Violet's movements, so that the
lovers were as totally separated by the
insurmountable barriers that conventional-

ism often raises, as though miles of land and sea had divided them from one another; but Eloisa and Abelard were not the only fortunate pair that rejoiced when

> " Heaven first taught letters for the wretch's aid,
> Some banished lover, or some captive maid."

CHAPTER III.

"Not Jove himself can now make void
    The joy that winged the flying hour;
The certain blessing once enjoyed
    Is safe beyond the Godhead's power.
Nought can recall the acted scene;
What hath been, spite of Jove, hath been!"

"Oh, love! oh, fire! once he drew
With one long kiss my whole soul through
My lips, as sunlight drinketh dew!"

Tennyson.

NFINITELY more dangerous to peace became the inter-views, perhaps doubly sweet because they were stolen; for what fruit

is so delicious on earth as the fruit that is forbidden? The meetings that were unsanctioned by the presence of parents, unwitnessed by the prying eyes of the world, could not be silent ones, and the burning words that Maurice had bravely restrained himself from uttering in the solitude of crowds and ball-rooms, burst involuntarily and vehemently from his lips, surrounded by sylvan shades, and with no one near him but the woman that he madly loved. He could have exclaimed with the poet—

"No eye to watch, and no tongue to wound us,
All earth forgot, and all heaven around us,"

as he stood with her clasped closely in his arms.

The two had not met for what, counting by Cupid's Almanac, was an eternity, though calculating the time by the com-

monplace method of seconds, minutes,
hours, and days, a fortnight might have
summed the period of probation. Any
way, the souls of both were literally
thirsting for a sight of one another,
just for one long look, one fervent hand-
clasp.

Chance favoured them at last, and
seizing the golden opportunity, Maurice
slipped into Vi's little palm a note, prepared ages before—a tiny billet, measur-
ing not more than a couple of inches in
circumference, but containing more en-
trancing food for the imagination than
the most romantic, closely written,
three-volumed novel, author ever pro-
duced.

The midnight hour, the hour in which
the outcast and the homeless prowl out,
together with the hardened felon that

shuns the light, and the wretched being
to whom that light is a hateful mockery.
Yet there was one who kept a tryst
in this hour, whose days had seen
far more of sunshine than of shade,
one whose ways were good and
pure, and whose breast harboured no
guile.

It was one of those sultry summer
nights when the vaulted sky is shadowed
by hazy clouds, with just here and there
a twinkling star shining down through
them. But even if, instead of this, the
heavens had been one mighty expanse
of " silver sheen," it would have been
almost impossible to distinguish the contour
of the form that glided, closely cloaked,
under the trees. All that could be seen
of the delicate apparition, was a pair
of bright dark eyes, restless as they

hurriedly glanced from side to side. A pair of eyes that *looked* a rendezvous.

Violet crept noiselessly along, with a step so wondrously light, that her tiny feet would hardly have dashed away the dew from a daisy, or bent the swaying stalk of the tenderest fern; and she started perceptibly like a guilty thing, at each low whisper of the west wind, at each trembling of a feathery spray in the breeze, and at each rustle of a fallen leaf, stirred by the trail of her training skirt.

The effort that it had cost her to go thus far alone, and at such an hour, was so great, that she sank half-fainting down upon the trunk of an old elm.

For an instant or so, she scarcely seemed to breathe, her cheek flushing, and her heart beating to suffocation. The impropriety of a meeting at the dead of night appeared to represent to her pure and fresh young mind the terrible aspect of a crime. She had but a short time before, in the sanctuary of her own bed-room, absolutely trembled with impatience to be where she was, and now she would have given the world never to have come!

She feared one instant that Maurice might fail in keeping the appointment; the next moment she dreaded his coming to find her waiting for him. What should she do? retrace her steps at once? Alas! she might never look upon him again if her resolution to return home was carried out, so—she stayed.

She looked very lovely on the lowly seat she had chosen; the moon was rising slowly higher and higher, and she sat bathed in a sheet of light. Oppressed with the sultriness of the night, she had unfastened her cloak, and it had partially fallen off her, revealing the white swan-like throat, and display-ing the symmetry of her figure. Her hat lay neglected by her, and in the restlessness of watching, she had pushed her hair aside, and escaping from the confining comb, the lustrous masses hung in undulating waves below her waist. With her white garments gleaming in the moonlight, and her hand like a snow-flake, pressed upon her breast, she looked like a " spirit from above that had wandered down to earth."

A step resounded on the turf, and for the very first time in her life, Violet was caught in her lover's embrace, with his lips against her cheek. "Imparadised in one another's arms," the rapid beating of their hearts was all the sound they heard, except that to amorous ears the gentle flutter of Cupid's wings might have been audible, as he flew through the air close by!

Maurice felt that the fairest creature the earth held, was his! upon his breast ; her long hair swept over him, she loved him, he alone occupied her heart! What more of happiness could life ever bring to him again? He was alone with her for the very first time,— he could gaze upon her beauty, with no stranger intermeddling with his joy, with no other eye feasting on the charms that his jealous soul had longed so many a time to hide away from all but himself,—and yet he restrained himself from many a word and look that might have too fully revealed the ardent feelings within him.

He had for this girl, unprotected and alone as she was, at an hour when all the tenderest feelings of his nature were aroused, and when all the surroundings were provocative of human passions, a sentiment that was of the purest and noblest kind.

He was close to her; the fragrance of her tresses,⸰ of her breath, swept over him, her luminous eyes gazed up into his so lovingly out of their frank depths, and he felt the sweet contact of her form; and yet an invisible distance divided them that he would not have dared, or even desired to encroach on, one step. Her youth, her innocence, her evident faith and love, were all-powerful pleaders

in her cause, and for their sake he kept
the strictest guard over his words and
actions lest they should lead him out of
himself.

It was wrong of him to have tempted
her there, but " sin itself lost half its evil,
by losing all its grossness."

"My dear one, my *own!*" he whispered, drawing her close to him, " but
a short time back, and I believed that
no love could stir my pulses, and now
I know that my heart lives and beats
as ardently as man's *can* do! Until I
saw *you* I was an infidel in affection.
It appears to me as if my past life
has been one long miserable prose—that
the poetry of existence is only opening
before me now !"

" Did you love me at first sight?" she
asked him, shyly.

"At once! It seemed as if my eyes and my heart went to meet yours in the very first glance! And should not love always come thus, instantaneously, spontaneously, my darling? But then it should also be overpowering and lasting as eternity itself! Oh, Violet! will eternal love be ours? It is now that I feel I really *care* to live. Until I knew you——but why should I speak of that wretched time — let the "dead past bury its dead." The future, with your presence to make sunshine for me, will atone for all I have suffered — for the bright illusions of boyhood rudely dispelled — for the lone and loveless life of many a weary year!"

And as his thoughts travelled back quickly in sad retrospection, his voice sounded almost painfully mournful to her ear.

"My dearest! if you only knew how sad a life mine has been, your womanly heart would plead for forgiveness for one who has, alas! no right to hold you thus! But it seems hard, terribly hard *always* to resist, when the thing you most long for on earth is within your reach! I have resisted to the utmost; I can do no more! I *want* your love, Violet—will you give it to me, in spite of anything that may happen—in spite of any barriers that may rise up between us?"

"In spite of anything, Maurice!" and she blushed rosy red as that name passed her lips for the first time.

"Do not look so sad, for I love you with all my heart, *dear* Maurice!" she said beseechingly, flinging her pretty arms round his neck, and forgetting her maidenly reserve in the natural desire of an honest true woman to see the man she loved happy.

"Maurice, *why* did you never tell me that you cared for me? It would have been far kinder, far better to have done so! It would have saved me so much pain, and then they might have known it at home, and we should not have been parted all this time! Why have you not spoken before? Tell me," she coaxed.

"My own, *don't* ask me! I cannot even now — I *dare* not tell you the exact truth. God knows it has been hard to keep my lips closed, when words of love for you were ever hovering upon them. But, Vi, we love one

another; can we live without each other?
Will you sacrifice a little for my sake,
will you consent to meet me *here* sometimes, and to keep our meetings concealed? Miserable circumstances, over
which I have no control *at present*, make
me ask this—beg this on my knees,"
and he threw himself before her and
grasped her two hands.

" *Will* you grant this, Violet? For
you *must* know that if it were otherwise,
not a day, not an hour should pass
before I claimed you openly before the
whole world!"

Poor Violet! She was a good and
well-principled girl, naturally averse to
everything that was underhand and
savouring of deceit, but she was like
wax in the grasp of the man she worshipped and believed in so implicitly,

and he could have moulded her to his slightest will. Upon his upturned face the "twin stars" shone down a perfect firmament of tenderness, and away from her memory flew the golden precepts of rectitude and truth that she had been taught so carefully, and trained in so strictly.

Love ruled—mighty, omnipotent—but with a sway so unutterably sweet that she never dreamed of resisting, and she murmured out in the low and cooing tones of a dove to its mate—

"It *is* wrong and very deceitful— but I *will* do whatever you ask, for I could not bear the misery *now* of never seeing you!"

The misery of absence would indeed be aggravated sevenfold, she thought, now that she had tasted of the " knowledge of good and evil," and had learnt that to lay her head on his breast, and to listen to the words that fell from his lips, was a fore-glimpse of a terrestrial paradise she had pictured, but never imagined really existed. Then came a recollection of her parents—their anger if her duplicity was discovered, and she asked anxiously—

"But it will not be for long, this concealment, Maurice?"

"No, dearest, not for long, God willing! The day may come sooner than we think when no silence will be necessary. Until then you will be true to me?—true to the very core?" he said, passionately, and she pressed closer to him in mute but earnest assent.

The moon grew larger and larger, and sailed in majesty above like a

gigantic Koh-i-noor upon the shifting
fleecy clouds, and the lovers looked up
at it, and felt their love increase each
moment, like the glorious planet. And
whilst it flooded all around with silver,
they traced its flickering light upon each
leaf, and indulged in the fond fancies
that naturally spring from such an hour.
Before they parted the summer dawn was
breaking, with a faint pink tinge just
here and there; and the birds, that had
been eavesdroppers to the murmured love
whispers were twittering amongst the
branches and flinging off the dew from
their glistening plumage.

"Maurice, have you *ever* loved any
other woman?" she asked.

Poor child, she did so thirst in that
most blissful hour of her life, for the
precious assurance that every really

loving woman craves for—namely, that the man she adores has never experienced in the past, the feelings that are his and hers, in the present.

Réchauffés never satisfy like fresh originals, no matter how much an expert hand may endeavour to flavour them, and render them palatable.

Maurice hesitated ere he replied; his conscience smote him sorely enough for having yielded to the temptation of meeting her, of avowing his love, and of receiving her sweet confession in return. He felt that he could not add deceit to the fault he had already committed, even though the deceit might be denominated mildly, a "white lie," an ignoring or diplomatic evasion of her question.

The simple, but heartfelt pathos of her

tone touched him to the heart. He
knew that all deception in the course of
life is "nothing but a falsehood reduced
to practice — a lie, passing from words
into things;" and he loved her far too
sincerely to allow her deliberately to
rest under any false impression.

Yet in spite of the occurrences of the
past, he knew his feelings for this girl
were no *réchauffés*, and that what he had
exaggerated and dignified as true "love"
before, had been nothing but a phantasm
of youth.

Taking her hands into his own, and looking steadfastly into the brown eyes, with an
expression that made their owner believe
implicitly every word he uttered, he said—

"*You* are my first love, and my last!
If you ever cast me off, never shall
woman on this earth, hear words of

affection from my lips. But you never *will* desert me, darling! You *will* cling to me? — have faith in me — and when the blessed time comes, belong to me, my dearest one! Promise me this, just once more before you go."

" I will always love you, and will be your wife whenever you ask me, Maurice—I swear it!"

" Then seal your oath thus, and thus," he said, kissing her lips for the first time during their interview, and feeling dreadfully guilty at his deed the while. What business had he to succumb to the weakness? Only, he could not deny himself just for once; when those lips were so near him, invitingly luscious as twin cherries ripened beneath southern skies, ready to be plucked, and yielding to his touch!

It *was* very wrong of him, but few men in his place would have resisted, even as he had done.

"May Heaven keep you for me, my own!" were the last words that kept ringing in Violet's little pink ears, as she fell asleep with a happy smile parting her lips, and a fervent prayer for her lover in her heart.

CHAPTER IV.

"UNCERTAIN, COY, AND HARD TO PLEASE."

"By those sweet eyes where light is ever playing,
    Where Love in depths of shadow holds his throne,
And by those lips which give whate'er thou'rt saying,
    Or grave or gay, a music of their own!
A music far beyond all minstrel's playing:
    I love but thee! I love but thee!

"By that fair brow where innocence reposes
    As pure as moonlight sleeping upon snow,
And by that cheek whose fleeting blush discloses
    A hue too bright to bless this world below,
And only fit to dwell on Eden's roses:
    I love but thee! I love but thee!"—*Moore.*

ELEVEN A.M., in the most perfect little bachelor's apartment in the world, commenc-
ing from the grey and gold-starred walls,

and rich oriental hangings, down to the
thick yielding Turkey carpet under foot.
The furniture of carved *bois de chêne*,
was an importation from Paris; some exquisite proofs of Landseer and Herring,
a statuette of Mercury by Thorwaldsen,
and another of Bacchus and Silenus,
besides one or two rare vases of old Buon
Retiro porcelain, adorned the room. A
huge tiger skin was spread before the
fireplace, and on it, extended at full
length, lay a magnificent deerhound. In
a luxurious arm-chair, with his feet rest-
ing upon the sleeping dog, lounged Arthur
Gordon.

"By Jove, I know she'll end by driving
me mad, stark, staring mad! It would
be easier to follow the caprices of a *feu
follet* than hers! Talk of the delusion of
a mirage! Why it's nothing compared

to her! and as to the tortuous windings
of her will, the evolutions of a serpent
would be a joke to them! Oh, Letty, I
owe you several! and if I ever have it
in my power to pay you out for ·the
dance you are leading me, I swear I'll
do it. She's such a dear, soft little
thing though, I think I would try what
effect love would have first! How nice
she looked last night !"

And as an appropriate accompaniment
to this last little "spoony" reflection, he
whistled a bar or two of—

" She danced like a fairy,
She sang like a bird."

"But how devilish ill she behaved
to me! Why *can't* I screw up enough
courage to ' put it to the touch and
win or lose it all,' instead of incessantly
dangling about *affiché*-ing my feelings

everywhere like a fool?" and in his impatience he struck the dog with his boot.

"Beg your pardon, Hector, old fellow! You are about the only thing that really loves me, I believe!" he sighed, stooping to pat the animal, who by way of showing his acceptance of the apology, licked his master's hand affectionately, and wagged his heavy tail slowly backwards and forwards, in a serious regal fashion that was peculiar to himself.

The grievance of the night before, on which Arthur was so bitterly ruminating, had consisted of a rebuff from Miss Lettice Grey, in one of her ordinary capricious fits.

He had hovered near her and her party for some length of time, anxiously awaiting a chance of a word, and longing yet fearing to approach the girl, when Mrs.

Smith, a kind-hearted though worldly woman, divining the state of his mind, suddenly remarked,—

"Letty, you have not been dancing much this evening, there's a set just forming, and Sir Arthur Gordon looks inclined to join it."

"Thanks, Janet dear, but I am very tired, and Mr. Terence has just offered to give me an ice," and the wilful fairy, casting a sly, triumphant glance at Arthur's crestfallen countenance, moved quietly away.

"It's no good — she is determined to avoid me, she positively *hates* me," murmured poor Gordon to himself, as he lit his cigar and sadly wended his way homewards.

The depression of the night was heavy upon him still, as he lay back with his eyes half closed, " chewing the cud of sweet and bitter fancy."

"Open Sesame!" exclaimed a clear ringing voice, and light-hearted, and fresh as a lark, Reggy Peel entered the room.

"Hallo! Arthur; what's up? Your face looks as blank as my account at my banker's! Hipped, eh?"

"No, not particularly. Have some breakfast?"

"Yes, I don't mind; why you haven't touched a thing! Try a glass of this Volnay, and some of these *côtelettes aux tomates*. They are first rate. They'll give you more stamina than that Soda and B, you seem to be imbibing. How did you amuse yourself last night?"

"Not much; there was no one worth speaking to scarcely."

"Did you see Miss Grey's new man? She took up with that fellow Terence, and seemed to have eyes for no one else. What can she see in him?"

"Yes, what *can* she see in him, or in all the other puppies that she takes up and puts down again, as if they were senseless dummies, and had no feelings whatever? she has no more heart than that chair there!" and he kicked the offending sample of Miss Lettice Grey's nature, and angrily and viciously champed away at the drooping ends of his moustache.

"She *is* a desperate flirt, and no mistake," asserted Reggy, adding in a commiserating tone, "I pity her husband if she ever has one!"

Arthur's blood boiled up to fever heat in a second.

"Talk of women's spite, why you fellows

beat them hollow! What on earth has Miss Grey done to rile you, that you should depreciate her like that?"

"Why, Arthur!"—and Reggy Peel, with his mouth full of *pâté de foie gras*, and his eyes wide open, stared at Gordon in astonishment.

"Oh! I see which way the land lies! forgive and forget, old chap, and accept the sincere wishes of your humble servant for success. Bless me, I have been blind as a mole, not to find out that the spell of other days was over you!"

The two men smoked away in silence for several minutes after this.

"What's become of Lynn, Arthur?"

"He was ailing, more in mind than body, I fancy, and has gone away for a few days' change."

"That accounts for the milk in the

cocoanut," as a vulgar old Puerto Rico Consul used to say in the F. O."

" I wondered why Miss Chesterton danced four times consecutively with Lord Harcourt. Is that to be a match? She does not look as if she cared one straw about him, and he has a little affair on hand elsewhere. A villa at Brompton, and a dark green brougham, with a tiny face with big blue eyes peeping out of it; but of course that needn't clash with a matrimonial alliance in high life. Cécile's steps tend towards Cremorne and the Argyle, and the future Lady Harcourt's dainty tread will be confined to more exclusive soil."

" It is lucky for the ambitious old Chestertons, that Lynn has taken himself out of the way at present."

" Rubbish, *mon cher*," ejaculated Gordon.

"Harcourt isn't a bad sort of fellow, although his morals may not be A 1, but he is much too *liéd* with *cocottes* to contemplate marriage. As for Maurice, he never went in for flirtation in his life —men of his calibre never do—they are in the habit of taking everything too much *au sérieux*. I would not mind wagering a good round sum that he never looked upon Vi Chesterton but as a beautiful clever girl, whose conversation is more edifying than half the 'Misses' one meets."

"If there is nothing beyond a commonplace sentiment between Lynn and Miss Chesterton, I am egregiously mistaken! Any one can see that she loves him, even by her eyes. But I must be off, and having reversed the adage of 'business first and pleasure afterwards,' I will tell you my principal reason for dropping in upon you this morning. Mrs. Smith— *Marmaduke* Smith I should say, for *la belle* Jeannette confided to me the other day, that without that euphonious *prénom*, her cognomen was perfectly odious to her, has sent you a little message. She gives a *fête champêtre* to-day at some tumble-down place that she calls " classic ruins;" the party are to meet at her house at three precisely, and she *particularly* desires your company. Will you go?"

" Perhaps, if I feel up to it by and by."

" Ta-ta, then, and *au revoir* I hope!"

* * * *

Punctually at three o'clock, Gordon reached the appointed rendezvous. He had fortified the inner man by a strong cup of coffee, and one or two *petits verres*, by the aid of which he had managed to pull his spirits up to the requisite pitch.

The *fête champêtre* was nothing more or less in itself, than the stereotyped picnic of all classes. A ramble over uncomfortable ground, detached couples whispering soft nothings behind a hedge, or within the shadow of a dilapidated archway, and groups of people, growing rapidly hilarious over frothy *Moët* and baskets of broken victuals. But if an insight into the hearts of the revellers had been feasible, the *fête* would have acquired far greater interest for the looker-on.

The hostess herself was a study, as she sat there comparing furtively and regretfully Reggy Peel's thoroughbred look and features, with the plebeian physiognomy of her vulgar but good-natured stockbroker, who, desirous of doing honour to the party, had donned the most flashy tie and waistcoat his wardrobe could supply, and who, suffering from the united effects of the summer sun and champagne, persisted in energetically passing over his rubicund visage a large yellow bandana, that was his wife's pet aversion. Lettice Grey, too, was in an unsociable mood. Her ordinary vivaciousness seemed to have entirely deserted her, and she appeared both bored and *préoccupée.*

It might have been chance, or a chance aided strongly by purpose, that made her creep stealthily away from the scene of festivity towards the woodland sequestered paths, where she amused herself by crowning her pretty brow with wild - flowers, until she impersonated the loveliest Ophelia in the world. She was not however doomed to waste her sweetness on the desert air.

Arthur had followed on her track, and was an admiring spectator of the picture she made.

In the sudden surprise of actually finding herself in close juxtaposition with her *ex-fiancé*, she forgot for an instant that they *had* quarrelled, and starting forward, she held out her hands towards him ; but the next moment recollecting the past, she dropped them again, and half averting her face, stood like a statue of Undine, waiting until her lover should with his voice and touch awaken the soul within her into life.

He was not tardy in obeying what both instinct and inclination bade him, and in a trice the girl's slight figure was in his arms, the flower - decked tresses lay on his bosom, and two pairs of lips ratified the contract of mutual forgiveness and an everlasting truce.

" Oh, Letty! it seems such a century of grief and pain since we parted," he whispered. " For Heaven's sake become my wife ere aught can separate us again!"

Lettice nestled up lovingly into his embrace, but pouted like a spoilt child.

" Not so fast, Arthur. You were very unkind, very cruel to me, and I have not forgiven you yet. I don't believe I ever shall."

"Not forgive me, my pet? Why it is *I* who ought to pardon you! But now, try not to be wilful for once in your life. In the first flush of my renewed happiness, *do* let me enjoy myself without any specks overhead. I am so happy, little woman!—happy as a king—holding you like this, and being allowed to——"

The rest of the sentence was indistinct, being " acted instead of spoken," and Letty had to submit, and was forced to cry *de grace!* before she was released.

"Arthur, promise *never* to be jealous or doubtful of me again."

"Never! I swear it, unless you make me so ; but never mind the past, darling, we have the present and the glorious future, and the sooner that future begins the better for *both* of us, I say ? or who knows but something may occur to dash away the cup of happiness from our lips a second time."

She was seated on the grass by this time, with Gordon half lying beside her. He held her hands firmly in his own, and Lettice, rosy and pale alternately, gazed down on the dear chestnut head, and longed to imprint a kiss on his clustering curls.

" Could you bear to part from me again?" he asked her.

" No, I could not;" and the lightness was gone from her tone. " You cannot have suffered more than I have, dear. I never forgot you for a moment."

" Then all your avoidance of me was
mere acting — your apparent dislike a
sham.   Oh, Letty!"   And he shook his
head gravely at her, but his eyes
laughed as they met her deprecating
glance.

" I am quite content *now*, any way,
that I know you are mine again, that
my eyes seem to see you and you only
in the world, that I am at your
feet, and that my existence is all
sunshine."

" Arthur, what syren has been teach-
ing you the art of making pretty
speeches?"

"No one but my own heart.   Look
here, Letty, I have never loved any
other but you.   I vowed, when you
discarded me, that no other woman
should ever have an influence over me;

besides what chance could any one have of gaining the heart that was filled with you, only you ?"

" And there is no one else you care for, Arthur, anywhere, in some little corner? Tell me," questioned the girl with a *moue mutine*, and with her breast heaving with the jealousy of a southern maiden.

" No one, dearest."

" 'Pon honour?"

" On my life!"

" I should *die* if there were," she said, passionately, with great flashing eyes. " I believe I should kill her, and you too! or neither, perhaps, but only myself," she added, in a sad little voice. All the flippant *répartee* that characterized her had died entirely out of her manner, and she only remembered the truth, the depth of her love for this man, whom she had so nearly lost for ever.

"My darling child!"—and after the custom of lovers, for awhile their discourse was completely made up of sweet phrases, of which tautology was the principal feature, and which a third party would inevitably have stigmatized as *bosh*.

"Arthur, they say that excess of happiness makes people very selfish; but I do not think that. Being so happy myself, I wish Violet was happy too! Poor girl, she was looking awfully ill yesterday; and sometimes, when I pop in suddenly, I find her eyes all full of tears; and there are tears in her voice as well when she answers sadly, 'Nothing,' in reply to my anxious questions. I cannot imagine why Mr. Lynn acts so very strangely."

"Maurice Lynn? Why, what on earth has he to do with Miss Chesterton's illness or happiness?"

"I am certain he cares for her; and yet he has never really proposed. He *must* see how she loves him, if only by her eyes!"

Gordon started. Letty had uttered almost the very same words as had fallen from Reggy Peel's mouth that very morning. Could there really be any foundation for an idea that he had scouted as ridiculous and improbable.

"Maurice care for Miss Chesterton, and propose to her! Why, you are dreaming! Lynn is a married man!"

"Married!" she cried. "Oh, how cruel, dishonourable of him, to have behaved

as he has done! Poor Vi, it will break
her heart to hear this! But who will
dare to tell her? And you, Arthur, you
must have surely seen what was passing,
and yet you never stretched out a saving
hand to her. Why did you not mention
a fact long ago, that every one here is in
ignorance of?"

"I was far too much occupied with
you, Letty, too perplexed and miserable
about my own troubles. I never thought
of Maurice as a lover; he is usually so
cold, so wrapt up in his books, and I
fancied he rather disliked women. Besides, he knew he was bound long ago,
and that some reason existed which pre-
vented him from having a divorce. You
must be making a mistake, my dear one;
I sincerely hope you are, or I shall never
forgive myself for having been the un-

fortunate medium of introduction between them."

"No mistake, but sad, sober, stern reality! I shall go home at once, Arthur. I could not stand the dancing and laughing at this fête, when I know what a fearful trial is in store for Violet. We were schoolfellows together, and have always been such close friends. She is so good, Arthur, and I am so sorry for her," she sobbed.

"Don't cry so, for mercy's sake, my pet, my little one; I cannot bear the sight of your tears. Nerve yourself to the task of telling her the truth; you will do it better than any one else. Let her be undeceived as soon as possible; and we must trust that pride or anger will give her strength to bear the blow bravely."

CHAPTER V.

MARRIED!

"When hope is chidden that fain of bliss would tell,
  And love forbidden in the breast to dwell;
    When fettered by a viewless chain,
    We turn and gaze, and turn again;
    Oh, death were mercy to the pain
      Of those who bid ' Farewell !' "
                              Heber.

"Eyes look your last, arms take your last embrace!"
                              Shakspeare.

HOT day, savouring almost of the Tropics, with the brilliancy of the blue sky unflecked and untempered by speck or

cloud, and only enough air stirring to waft the scent of the summer flowers into a pleasant room, whose green jalousies were partially closed to exclude the garish noon. A charming *demi-jour* light fell on richly gilded jardiniers heaped over with various freshly cut blossoms; on costly tables loaded with expensive *bric-à-brac;* on soft downy cushions fashioned in Eastern looms; and numerous objects of *virtù*, denoting considerable wealth, with the ofttimes unusual accompaniment of a pure and refined taste. The walls were of a delicate cream colour, panelled in dead gold; a few choice oils embellished them here and there. One or two rare bronzes and some priceless specimens of old china adorned the white marble mantelpiece, and a couple of huge mirrors in elaborately carved frames, placed

within opposite niches, reflected the whole
of the interior of the apartment, as
well as the form of its sole occupant.

At one end of a luxurious lounge
half-reclined Vi Chesterton. A book lay
carelessly in her lap, open; but had a
curious observer peeped over her shoulder
at its contents, they would have been
puzzled to decipher letters that were
upside down—even the pages were uncut,
although the girl's dainty fingers played
restlessly with an ivory paper-knife, with
the blade of which she unconsciously
turned over leaf after leaf of the
volume.

Her head was bent slightly downwards
and her eyes were completely veiled under
their thick lashes, as though she did
not care to reveal their tell-tale glances
even to the mirror opposite. Every now

and then she sent a rapid furtive look towards the casement, at each sound of a twig fluttering against the sill, or a human footfall on the gravel paths of the garden.

Since the ball at which Maurice had first seen her, she was strangely altered. She had suffered from the million hopes, fears, and uncertainties attendant on Love, so erroneously apostrophized as the divine passion, when to most mortals it presents oftener the torments of Inferno.

Violet's countenance, that was wont to be characterized by a calm and regal type of loveliness — lacking perhaps, in the estimation of many, a sufficient mobility of feature in its rigidly classical contour—had lost its erewhile serenity, and in lieu of a want of animation showed various expressions flitting quickly across the pretty red lips and shining out of the great dark eyes.

She looked a little pale and wan too, even a shade older, and her figure was not so full as of yore, though none the less symmetrical and graceful.

The warm summer afternoon had lagged wonderfully on its course to her, in spite of its beauty and brightness, as she sat there alone intently listening with a strained ear, and impatience in her breast, for a tread which to her bore upon it the " music of the spheres." Her people were absent, and she had, after much hesitation and wavering, yielded to her lover's earnest solicitations, to give him a rendezvous at her own house.

The fact was that their meetings had somehow become far more difficult to compass than they used to be in earlier days. Fate seemed to have set its face dead against them, and no sooner was an interview arranged than some circumstance cropped up, as it were on purpose to prevent its taking place.

The house was built in villa fashion, with long French windows opening down to the lawn, and it was through one of these that Maurice would come. She sat still as a marble statue of patience, outwardly. Inwardly, her heart was beating fast, and exaggerating the length of each winged moment into hours, as she looked hurriedly at the tiny jewelled watch at her side, and marvelled at the snail-like progress of time on this particular day.

Over the stone ledge of the window stepped at length a foot, but not *his*; and she started up, annoyed at the untimely intrusion, to feel Letty's cold hands clasping hers, and Letty's unusually pallid face, with a sad and almost scared expression in her blue eyes, looking piteously into her own.

"What is it?" she exclaimed, whilst a firm conviction came over her that, if ill news was at hand, it must of necessity relate to the one beloved object on whom every feeling and thought she had, turned.

"Nothing, dear; nothing! Now, please sit down, and let me talk to you."

"Cannot you come a little later?" Vi stammered, blushing rosy red, and feeling terribly unmaidenly and guilty as she asked the question.

"I am anxious to be alone just now," she pleaded, coaxingly; then seeing her companion disinclined to move, she summoned up courage to speak more decidedly, fancying that each moment might bring *him.*

"Do not be angry, Letty, but indeed I *must* be alone now."

"Alone, Vi? What for? If it is to see Mr. Lynn, you cannot ever see him again!"

"*Never* see him again! What *is* the matter? What has happened? Speak, Letty. He is not ill or hurt?"

"Far worse!"

"Not *dead*," she shrieked out, throwing herself down on her knees, and catching nervously at her friend's arm.

"No, no, not dead, Vi; but you must look upon him as dead to *you.* You must see him as he really is— worthless, dishonourable, deceitful; a man to be shunned by you—despised!"

"I think your senses must have left you, or you would never speak to me like this," Violet said, coldly and deliberately, rising slowly from her kneeling position, and drawing up her figure to its full queenly height, whilst her eyes flashed down scornfully and even a little contemptuously at Maurice's defamer.

"Do you know *how* I love him ?—reverence him, worship him ?—and yet you dare,— yes, Letty, 'dare' *is* the proper word for me to use, although you may resent it,—to breathe such bitter words as worthless, dishonourable, in conjunction with his name! Are you leagued with all the rest to vilify him in my eyes? It is useless! for these eyes will be fast closed within the grave before I credit one foul slander of the man

who has *deigned* to let me love him,
and to love me in return!"

"Do you know what this man has
done? He has deceived you by his
looks, by his tones, even if he has failed
in courage to utter lies! He has
made you believe in his truth and
honesty, when his life is one long
falsehood! Violet, you *must* give him
up!"

"Never! so help me Heaven!" the
girl said, determinedly, whilst her lip
curled at the very suggestion of infi-
delity to any woman who had once
loved Maurice, or been cared for by
him. "So long as he is true to me,
I will be true to him. Nothing on
earth but his own will can ever sever
us."

"Vi, you know my only desire is for

your happiness. I should be the last
to hurt you by maligning the man you
care for. *Believe* me, he does not deserve
your affection, dear;" then, seeing an
incredulous smile on Violet's face, she
added, hastily, "Oh, Vi, forgive me, but
I *must* tell you,—Maurice Lynn is a married man !"

"Married! My God!" and poor Violet
fell like a crushed flower to the ground,
insensible.

The next moment the footfall for
which she had listened so eagerly, and
longed for so earnestly, but to which
her ear was deaf now, echoed on the
garden-path and crossed the room with
hurried steps, and Maurice Lynn, with
astonished wonderment depicted on every
feature of his face, blanched as a spectre's,
lifted up his love, and held her on his

breast, whilst Lettice with trembling fingers sought restoratives for her aid.

" What ails her, Miss Grey ? Tell me, I beseech of you," interrogated poor Lynn, aghast, as he noted Letty's averted countenance, and watched breathlessly, but vainly, for the colour to revisit Violet's cheek, and the light to come back to her eyes.

" You had better leave at once before she revives," she answered him, curtly and angrily, as she glanced compassionately at her friend. " Poor girl, how she suffers ! You have almost killed her by your cruelty !"

" My cruelty ! Great Heavens ! what *do* you mean, Miss Grey ? Be explicit, I pray you ! Cruelty ! *I*, who would willingly sacrifice every hope on earth to give her the smallest happiness ! what have I done ? but love her— adore her, as all *must* do," he said, passionately.

" Oh, speak to me just one word, Vi, my darling — my own !" he implored, whilst he chafed her icy hands, and pressed her inanimate form vehemently against him, and even imprinted a long and fervent kiss on the pale brow lying upon his shoulder, callous to, if not forgetful of, Letty's very presence in the room.

After a little time she revived, but it had been infinitely better for her to have died in that trance, than to have awakened to find her life a misery — her love a crime.

And she spoke to him at last the words he had begged for; but she spoke

them in a voice that he could scarcely
realize as the one that had so often
and so tenderly breathed sweetest love-
words to him — a voice harsh, almost
stern, uncompromising in its accents,
hard as adamant in its ring. Drawing
herself slowly and shiveringly away from
his retaining embrace, she essayed to re-
gain her calmness, and strove to stand
erect and firm, but her figure swayed
in spite of her efforts, and she was forced
to lean upon Letty, who clasped her
affectionately, and in whose eyes great
shining drops gathered as she marked
the real suffering of the two before
her.

"Maurice, is it true that you are
married ?" And poor wretched Violet
bent upon him a long, steady, and
harrowing gaze that seemed to look

him through and through, and to question and to crave for a denial to her question, with a mute but intense pathos and pleading in the once radiant, proud eyes, like the dying glance of a dumb animal stricken down by the very hand that had hitherto caressed it.

No answer came. Maurice was silent perforce, for the only words that he could utter, and which would be corroborative of the miserable truth, seemed to cleave to his mouth, and he vainly essayed to articulate them; and yet what could have been more painfully convincing to the girl than this very failure of speech?

He who asserted that small griefs can speak, but that great ones render us dumb, knew the human heart well.

Just for one second Maurice bowed
his head down on the sofa near him,
and almost appeared to cower as if in
shame at the discovery of his long
deception ; but the next moment he
looked up with a valiant effort to explain, and found that Letty had noiselessly vanished from the scene, leaving
Violet standing alone. A rapid move-
ment, and he was before her, clasping
her hands, pleading eagerly for pardon
as for dear life—gazing passionately,
pitifully upon the white cheek, the lips
quivering with an intensity of emotion
that she bravely strove to conceal, the
eyes so touchingly mournful, with pupils dilated by unshed tears, and yet
filled with a sort of resolute light as
they sadly confronted his own. But
he had only to look at her to know

that the death-blow to her happiness
had failed to annihilate her love; that
she was still unchanged; that the resolute spirit was but transitory; that his
delinquencies had not dispossessed him
of his power to turn at will the
marble image of beauty before him
into a creature of flesh and blood, rife
with warmth and feeling; and that by
the mere contact of his touch he could
tint its pale features with a deep
crimson tide.

He recalled to himself a thousand
deliciously-whispered assurances that she
had breathed, pledging herself to him
in spite of anything that could occur;
and he could not persuade himself that
her pride and determination would
prove dominant over the love that she
had so often fully and freely vowed,

and he had so implicitly believed in.
He would trust to the mightiness of
that love now ; he *must* trust to it,
for it was the only thing left to him
to cling to, in the maelstrom of misery
in which he was shipwrecked. He
knew, and the knowledge was sweet
balm to him too, that though he must
seem in her eyes to have acted vilely,
yet she would never fail to hold out
to him a saving hand, and if she
could do so, would land him in a
haven of safety and peace.

They loved one another, and it would
be death to part. Should he ask her,
now that she knew everything, to go
away with him, to forego the sanction
of her parents, to defy the world, to
leave her home with all its associations
of innocence and happiness, to share

his fortunes in another land? His own, and his only; worshipped and waited on by him as never empress was before; adored more than woman had ever been; but still with her proud brow, that a diadem would have suited, branded with the fatal brand of infamy, her purity blasted, her life a daily lie, her name unblessed by the holy title of "wife!"

Should his be the cruel hand to hold to her lips the "cup of doubtful bliss" that must be drunk by those who believe in "all for love, and the world well lost?" When such terrible trials might await her at each turn, could he let his dear one, his innocent darling, run the gauntlet with the world's fierce scorn, and stand meekly by to see her spirit first wounded, then crushed, by perpetual slights, repulsed by all, rebuked by many a scoffing word or covert sneer? Could he make up his mind to submit tamely to the bitterness of her humiliation, of knowing that, with all her peerless beauty and angelic nature, she would fall immeasurably lower in the social scale than the Messalinas of society who never hesitated to break the holiest ties for the gratification of passion or vanity, but who erred secretly, managing to cast a mantle of outward respectability over their sins ? Could he survive the horrible torture of feeling that, though his breast would pillow her head, his love would be powerless to insure peace to her heart?

It was true that he had learnt to idolize her; that he had garnered up his soul in her; that she had become part and parcel of his existence; that her smile made him forget that Heaven existed not upon this earth!

He cursed bitterly, for her dear sake, the weakness that had taken hold of him, now that he was fully and most painfully awakened to a sense of what *would* have been right and honourable. He knew that he ought to have left her whilst her affection was yet young; trusting that in the trials of absence the love that had only blossomed for him, might expand into flower for some happier man than himself; but it was not too late to make the sole amends that lay in his power, to leave her at once, and prevent all further sacrifice on her part for him. He never remembered though that his self-abnegation came but tardily, that he had seared her heart with a wrong no other hand would be capable of erasing from it. He determined on going away at once, broken-hearted, but alone, trying to believe that "all was not utter darkness, because a black cloud overcast the sky —that when the gloom is most dense the brightness of the morn is nearest at hand;" but before he went he would have her pardon, nay even a reiteration of the love that in this hour seemed more precious than ever to him.

"I *have* acted vilely—wickedly!" he began, in deprecating accents, "but *don't* condemn me unheard! Listen to me for one moment, my darling! Have I indeed been so much to blame that my heart *would* cling, in spite of me, to you? That I yielded myself up at length to a passion that I had in fact from the very first lost all real power to stem or control? A passion a thousand times stronger than myself! That I gave the reins after many struggles, the magnitude of which none can tell, to a feeling that I *ought* to have curbed and tamed. *Ought!* How easily said, how seldom done! A feeling that swept away by its depth and violence all recollection of honour and rectitude. I only remembered *you!* Oh, my own, I should have been more than mortal if I had possessed sufficient moral strength to sever with my own hands, by my own will, the link that has lately bound my life to all that could give it hope and joy. But although I have treated you horribly, I don't ask for mercy, or for pardon; I want your heart to pay back the deep and undying love that fills mine! And you do not hate me even now, Vi! Though I deserve all your hatred and scorn to the uttermost, you even care for me still! I *feel* it; I see it in your dear face, your eyes, in the cold clamminess of these poor little hands that feel my kisses on them for the last time! Think, Vi! for the *very last time !*"

"No more of this, I beg of you," she whispered, in broken tones, trying to withdraw her hand from him, but her voice had quite lost its hard adamantine tone, and her accents were breathed in a low soft cadence, full of saddest music, that sounded like a dirge for lost happiness! "I have been tried enough: I can bear no more," and the hands grew more icy still, that he held in his strong clasp, whilst big tears welled up fast, dimming her vision, and she endeavoured to avert

14---2

her face, to hide its agitation from him.
"Oh, Maurice, let me go, I beseech of
you! for we *must* part now and for
ever!"

"Not yet, not yet, for God's sake, Vi!"
he exclaimed ; and as the thought came
to him, of the arid waste his existence
would become when she was gone out of
it, his voice grew hoarse and troubled.
"Darling, just think how many long
and weary years we may both have to
pass, and do not try to shorten the
space of this one little hour! Tell me
that you will strive, at any rate, not to
think too harshly of me; that the very
extent and madness of my love for you
will in some measure plead its excuse,
for I *do* love you, Violet, more, I think,
than man ever loved woman before! I
know it is very wrong of me to ask it,

but Heaven will surely pardon me for the sake of the long suffering, the terrible expiation I have before me! But I want you to lay your head just once more down upon my breast, and to put your lips upon mine, and say 'Good-bye' to me there! God knows my future lowers dark and gloomy enough. Do not grudge me the memory of a last caress. Let a happy vision of these moments rise up to cheer my lonely life sometimes! I *may* 'belong,' as it is called, to another woman, but you know that I am yours to all eternity; that I shall *never* know another love! Child, *don't* turn away from me: it cuts me to the very heart! You *cannot* surely be grown hard and cruel in so short a time?"

"I do forgive you; I am not hard or cruel," she tried to articulate.

" Then give me one kiss—one fond word
—that I may carry their memory as my
only comfort into the world where,
perhaps, we two shall never meet again!
Think what a world that will be to me,
and that death were a million times pre-
ferable to the life of a living corpse; a life
that can own not one single moment of
happiness, bereft of the only thing that
could bring it warmth and light, the sunshine of our love. I have erred deeply ;
I know it; but my punishment is adequate
to my fault. *You* will not, you cannot,
add one grain to the already overflowing
measure of my misery. Once more, only
once more, Vi, tell me that I am dear
to you in spite of all !"

She had listened to him, silently, intently, trying to take in his words as they
fell from his lips; but her brain was in

a whirl, and her heart was beating to suffocation. She could only realize to herself that they must part; that a dreadful barrier had suddenly arisen between her and him; that their love must be stifled ere it became a greater sin. It seemed to her as though life had come to an end, and a grave, but a grave with a consciousness of its attendant horrors, was yawning at her feet.

"Maurice was another woman's husband !" she kept repeating to herself. These few but terrible words were her death-warrant, condemning her to leave all that life owns of happiness, for a desolate, loveless existence for the remainder of her days.

He was another woman's husband, and yet he dared to kneel before her, to insult her by breathing such words as

he was doing! In the world's censorious
eyes, what a contemptible position she
must hold! Ah, what had she done to
merit falling so low, to have been marked
out, in the fulness of her pride, as an
object for an unlawful passion—a married
man's plaything, to be toyed with for
awhile only—to be cast aside later;—to
have been led into revealing openly, un-
reservedly as she had done, how entirely
a forbidden love filled her every pulse!

No, she would never utter one
phrase of tenderness to him again—this
man, who was worthless, base; who had
sacrificed every proper feeling to his own
inordinate selfishness, to his insane and
insolent fancy for herself; who had held
her up as a target for malicious shots from
all around! He should not dare ever
again to contaminate her by his presence,

or pollute her by his touch, but tearing his image ruthlessly away from her, she would be brave and strong, and learn to look upon him at length with the indifference that duty rigidly extorted from her. "Kiss him just once again!" Why, he must indeed be stark, staring mad to ask it, she thought, when the very kisses that were past and gone, seemed even now to be burning upon her brow, and scorching her lips like coals of living fire, recalling vividly to her mind the shame those kisses had been to her—the dishonour of him who had given them! She would nerve herself up at once to be properly calm and cold; to say her final words quietly and firmly: that all her puny miserable efforts to hate him, for which she disdained herself, might be effectually hidden from him; that her pride might not suffer more by his pity; that he might not scorn the soft womanliness that her deep wrong had failed to destroy; that he might be compelled to respect the Spartan fortitude that could smile, whilst life itself appeared to her, to be ebbing in agony away!

And then she turned and looked upon him.

"The quicksands are not more easily changed by the wind, nor are the leaves more readily whirled by the winter's blast, than woman veers in her wrath."

Vi looked at him steadfastly for a moment, and her breath came quick, and her cheek crimsoned all over as she saw him there, crouching at her feet, more like a slave or a criminal, than a libertine exulting over his victim, or a conqueror regarding his captive.

His eager eyes, lifted up with such a wan, haggard, hungered expression in them, craving with a silent prayer for a loving glance from her. His face, whose every feature was indelibly engraved on her heart, so set, so drawn, with the concentrated misery of the last short hour—the brow, usually haughty, unruffled, contracted in pain — was it strange that her whole soul suddenly melted in divine pity and love?

What could be the world's verdict to her, an evil spirit whispered, weighed in the balance with his smallest good or happiness? What could *anything* be to her in comparison with the *everything* that he had become? What right had she, weak, erring creature as she was, to set herself up as his judge, to blame him for having succumbed to a love

whose power at this very moment was
omnipotent over herself! Her eyes returned him loving glance for glance;
warm, tender kisses, but pure as undriven snow in their source, rained down
upon his brow; and with her *world*
within the circle of her arms, he became
again her all in all. She realized the
perfect impossibility of tearing herself
away from him; she felt that she could
not doom herself deliberately to the torture of separation; she *dared* not face
an existence in which he would form
no part. What could life be worth if
its best element were wanting? How
could she get through the weary, lagging
days of absence, when that absence must
endure for ever? To fly with him, whom
she loved so utterly, without any home
blessings; pursued, perhaps, by a parental

curse, was a terrible prospect; but the thought that to go with him, to belong to him for ever whilst she lived; to see him daily, hourly; to devote to him the best energies of her heart and brain, and to know that he lived for her, and her love alone; conjured up such a vision of bewildering bliss, that she lost herself in its ecstasy, believing that she was his, to do with as he deemed best; that her future depended on his will! But such a delirium of feeling was but ephemeral, and utterly foreign to her right-thinking nature. Her better angel resumed its sway, and she became her own true self again.

But though conscience was awakened, and she was brave to do her duty, love for him was not lessened one iota in her heart, and compassion filled the place from which a temporary ebullition of anger had a few moments before, banished it.

"Maurice—dear Maurice!" she whispered, agitatedly, "have pity upon me. Save me from myself! Strengthen me in what is right, and leave me while yet I have the sense, the power, to bid you go! It *is* a sin to say so, but you are more to me than all the world. My very soul is yours! Not an hour of the day but you are in my thoughts; not a night but I see you in my dreams. The present is a wretched blank—the future will be a long, lingering torture; the past only is precious to me, for it is filled by you! Oh, my darling one! I *do* forgive you and love you still! Never shall I cease loving you! but I am looking upon you now as though death were dividing us for ever. God guard you always, my own dear Maurice, and bring you the happiness that *I* shall never feel again!"

She wound her arms passionately round his neck, holding him to her as though nought should separate them more. Then she gave him one long long pressure from her lips on brow and eyes and mouth, and was gone—leaving him alone, not only where he stood, but in the wide wide world!

CHAPTER VI.

PARTED.

"I found her not! The chamber seemed
Like some divinely haunted place
Where fairy forms had lately been,
And left behind their odorous trace!"
*　　*　　*　　*　　*
"It felt as if her lips had shed
A sigh around her as she fled!"
*　　*　　*　　*　　*
"Oh, my sweet mistress, where art thou?
In pity fly not thus from me;
Thou art my life, my essence now,
And my soul dies of wanting thee!"
Moore.

MAURICE stood where she had left him, stunned; then all at once his mind seemed to take in, with wonderful avidity, the whole of the terrible reality. The blow had indeed fallen, dashing away in one rapid swoop the cup of delicious nectar from his lips, demolishing in a tiny second the whole fabric of happiness that he had so carefully built up around him during the last few months of his life.

And yet, could he wonder at the sudden demolition of a fabric, slight and intangible, shadowy in its nature, with nothing but dishonour and falsehood as the basis on which it had been erected?

The veil, which he had so carefully striven to draw over the hideousness of his past, had not been gently lifted aside, so as to reveal gradually—piece by piece, as it were—to his dear love's gaze, all that he had wished so strenu-ously to conceal from her knowledge.

No time had been given him to explain to her assuredly sympathizing ear and pitying heart the extenuating circumstances of his case—the undeserved misery his antecedents had entailed, and the immense magnitude of the temptation which she in herself had presented, to prompt him to a course of apparent deceit, sooner than to lose for ever the sunshine of his existence—her presence; but the veil had been wrenched asunder rudely, as it seemed; allowing him neither hope nor opportunity of clearing himself to a certain extent in the eyes and estimation of the only being upon earth, whose continued affection and good opinion were infinitely more precious to him than food and raiment!

She was gone from him, never to return! and she had taken with her everything that made life valuable to him. All in that room where he stood seemed to speak of her—the impress of her form against the cushioned sofa; the open book flung on a chair close by; the scattered petals of the flowers, in the arrangement of which she had essayed to pass away the lagging hours until he came; the very breath of the wind stealing in at the open lattice, that had so lately kissed her cheek! Her voice came to him again in the fragrance of violets that rose from a little laced handkerchief, lying neglected on the floor at his feet. Stooping, he seized it, and covered it with mad kisses, as though it had been a living, breathing thing. It was all that was left to him of her! Then, hastily thrusting it into his breast, he left the house, and with rapid steps

pursued the first quiet road that led out
of the town.   He walked on and on,
unmindful of time or of physical fatigue;
he knew not whither — he cared not
where.

What was, in fact, anything, everything to him, now that Violet had given
him up?   For was

> " She not his life,
> The ocean to the river of his thoughts, that terminated
>   all ?"

It did appear so fearfully hard to him
that his whole happiness should be a
holocaust to that one miserable act of
his life—that he should suffer so terribly for the sin of another—for he knew
that he had been more sinned against
than sinning in that wretched fatal episode of his youth.   In all the many years
that had gone by since that autumnal

day, when he had gone down on his knees
and sworn to God, in the enthusiastic
fervour of boyhood, never to break by
his own will the vows he had breathed
at the altar; when he had implored the
help of Heaven to aid him in keeping
the oath that, whilst *she* lived, no other
woman should fill her place, he had
religiously endeavoured to avoid all
temptations that might lead him into
infringing that oath even in spirit. Since
that autumnal day he had been haunted
continually by the face and form of her
who had so utterly ruined his life; amidst
the gayest scenes, at every feast, like
the Egyptian skeleton, veiled and chap-
letted with funereal flowers, she had
seemed to sit for ever at his side, scaring
away by her dark presence everything
that savoured of joy or light.

Just for the space of a few short
months, when he had drunk deeply of
love at one glance—when love's glamour
had completely blinded his vision and
bewildered him with its ecstasy—when
love's elixir had steeped his senses in
temporary oblivion, and lulled him into
an Elysian dream—the miserable spectre
of the past had faded out of mind, and
left him free for a little while to revel
in all that life holds of hope and happiness.   But now it was back again at
his side once more, clinging to him tena-
ciously, binding his hands more closely
than ever with cankering, loathsome chains,
mocking at him with its well-remembered
taunting smile, flashing its strange eyes
into his face, and reminding him, in
the harsh discordant accents of old,
that he was still a fettered man!

And a poor consolation it was that all this misery had come to him for the sake of a transient passion. Alas! alas! Why had he not remembered in time that "passions are the gales of a man's life, and that it should be his care not to let them rise into tempests."

Just as one loves to look upon the pretty wavelets and the white surf of the sea dancing gently towards the shore, until suddenly, the wind rising, the tiny waves become lashed into furious billows, that dash over and submerge one, so he had gazed too long and too curiously, and toyed with the attractive emotions of a new and inviting pleasure, until it had first fascinated him, then imprisoned his feet and swept him into destruction.

It was summer time, and the country into which Maurice had wandered was enlivened by the season of haymaking. Brightly in the sunshine gleamed the brown, ruddy countenances of the reapers, whilst their merry peals of laughter kept ringing through the air; the subtle scent of the new-mown hay, united to the scent of an adjacent clover-bed, came wafted on the wings of the wind. The luxuriant verdure in which the fields had lately been clothed had yielded to the ruthless scythe, but around lay big bunches of flowers, all bruised under feet, but still emitting dying odours as a sweet and lingering farewell to the bright earth they were leaving for ever.

But Maurice was in no mood to admire the beauties of nature. The

clover-bed, showing up a silvery aspect
of green, interspersed with the rich hue
of its manifold blossoms, on which the
busy bees feasted to satiety, possessed
no possible attraction for him; and his
glance never wandered towards the tall
hedgerows, through which purple buds,
intermixed with snowy petals, peeped
gaily out. The corn shone yellow in
the sunlight, the dark shades of the
sycamores mingled with the tender
emerald foliage of the stalwart oaks
and elms, "and from the soft vernal
sky overhead, down to the grassy turf
at his feet, there was beauty around
him," but touching him as little as
though he were instead in the Great
Desert of Sahara, surrounded by arid
wastes and sandy plains.

For his " soul was sick even unto

death," and his brain thoroughly upset; doubts and fears had created a havoc within it that he deemed himself power-less to bring again into reasonable order; his heart was one chaotic space; he felt that—

"'Tis not the whole of life, to live,
Nor all of death, to die!"

There was only one question he kept reiterating again and again to himself: "Had happiness eluded his grasp for ever?" And in this, the first hour of Violet's loss, no power on earth could have called up a shadow of a belief that he would ever experience an emo-tion of joy again while he lived.

As he soliloquized mournfully, lean-ing against a stile that separated the meadow in which he stood from a small stream that swept along, with

tiny force and a gentle murmur, over
the big shining pebbles that lay in its
course, his eyes rested dreamily on the
clear water, vaguely pursuing the career
of the little objects that floated on the
surface. Suddenly the idea struck him
that, following the example of some one
he had read of, he would constitute
one of those floating trifles his fate,
and, paltry as it was, allow its
evolutions to govern the current of his
thoughts. He was far too miserable to
be wise; he wanted something, no
matter how trivial, to decide for him,
whether he should succumb to the
Fates, that seemed to have set their
faces dead against him, or whether he
should encourage " Hope," that might give
him sufficient strength to grapple manfully with the positive despair and des-

peration that appeared likely to over-
whelm him, deadening his faculties, and
reducing him to a misery which was
almost stupifying.

In the midst of his grief, the utter
absurdity of letting his reason be swayed
by such trivialities struck him with a
keen sense of ludicrousness, and brought
a bitter smile to his lip ; but still he
determined to pursue the idea, and not
to swerve from the rules laid down for
the somewhat original trial of destiny. So
he tracked one particular straw in its
progress; there was an angle in the
bank close by, and he made a vow that
that straw should be the umpire to
decide between hope and despondency
—that according to its safe passage, or
otherwise, round the diminutive promon-
tory, he would have weal or woe !

Gordon had said, "*Vive la Bagatelle!*" and he had ironically, and even a little commiseratingly received the sentiment, believing that it did discredit to his friend's heart and brain; and now in this moment, a mere bagatelle seemed everything in the world to him, so absurdly superstitious he felt in his anxiety to find an omen of good. He stood and watched the "pilot-boat" with eager eyes and throbbing breast, ashamed of himself, and yet he could not have turned away his gaze for a second to save his life. It enchained his glance as though it had been a basilisk, as it came gently down the stream, and he ejaculated, after the manner of the model he had chosen, "*Bonum velis !*"

It passed quickly on, now and then it met with a slight obstruction, but the stoppage was but momentary. "It doubled the cape — the Cape of Good Hope," as it was to him; and foolish Maurice, heaving a sigh of positive relief, "for love will subsist on wonderfully little hope," retraced his steps homewards, with a lighter heart, and sat down to write Violet a letter.

END OF VOL. I.

TINSLEY BROTHERS'
LIST OF NEW BOOKS.

The Gaming Table, its Votaries and Victims, in all
Countries and Times, especially in England and France. By ANDREW
STEINMETZ, Barrister-at-Law. 2 vols. 8vo.

Peasant Life in Sweden. By L. LLOYD, author
of " The Game Birds of Sweden." 8vo. With Illustrations.

The Battle-fields of Paraguay. By Captain R. F.
BURTON, author of "A Mission to Dahomé," "The Highlands of
Brazil," &c. 8vo. With Map and Illustrations.

Memoirs of Sir George Sinclair, Bart., of Ulbster.
By JAMES GRANT, author of "The Great Metropolis," "The Religious Tendencies of the Times," &c. 8vo. With Portrait. 16s.

Travels in Central Africa, and Exploration of the
Western Nile Tributaries. By Mr. and Mrs. PETHERICK. With
Maps, Portraits, and numerous Illustrations. 2 vols. 8vo, 25s.

Rome and Venice, with other Wanderings in Italy,
in 1866-67. By GEORGE AUGUSTUS SALA, author of " My Diary in
America," &c. 8vo, 16s.

The March to Magdala. By G. A. HENTY, Special
Correspondent of the *Standard.* 8vo, 15s.

Lasting Memories; being Personal Reminiscences
of Eminent Men. By GEORGE HODDER. 8vo.

The Enchanted Toasting-fork : a Fairy Tale. By
the Author of " Out of the Meshes." Profusely illustrated and hand-
somely bound. 5s.

The Rose of Jericho; or Christmas Rose. Translated from the French. Edited by the Hon. Mrs. NORTON.

TINSLEY BROTHERS, 18 CATHERINE STREET, STRAND.

TINSLEYS' MAGAZINE,

An Illustrated Monthly, price One Shilling,

CONTAINS:

GEORGE CANTERBURY'S WILL. A Serial Story. By
Mrs. HENRY WOOD, author of "East Lynne," &c.

AUSTIN FRIARS. A New Serial Story. By the Author of
"George Geith."

&c. &c. &c.

The first Five Volumes of TINSLEYS' MAGAZINE *are now complete,
price 8s. each. Cases for Binding may be had of the Publishers, or
through any Bookseller, 1s. 6d. each.*

MEMOIRS OF THE LIFE AND
REIGN OF GEORGE III.

WITH ORIGINAL LETTERS OF THE KING, AND OTHER
UNPUBLISHED MSS.

By J. HENEAGE JESSE, author of "The Court of
England under the Stuarts," &c.

3 vols. 8vo. £2 2s. Second Edition.

"The very nature of his subject has given these volumes peculiar
interest."—*Times.*

"Here, however, we must part with Mr. Jesse, not without renewed
thanks for the amusement which he has given us."—*Quarterly Review.*

"Mr. Jesse's volumes are brimful of amusement and interest."—
Spectator.

"Mr. Jesse's book is one to be eagerly read and enjoyed to a degree
rarely experienced in the perusal of English memoirs."—*Morning Post.*

"Nor do we hesitate to recommend the result of his labours to general
even more than to studious readers, satisfied that whilst unconsciously
imbibing instructive information they will be carried along from chapter
to chapter by a keen sense of intense and unflagging amusement."—
Daily Telegraph.

TINSLEY BROTHERS, 18 CATHERINE STREET, STRAND.

TINSLEY BROTHERS'
SERIES OF SEVEN-AND-SIXPENNY WORKS.

HANDSOMELY BOUND IN BEVELLED BOARDS.

Maxims by a Man of the World. By the Author
of " Lost Sir Massingberd."

The Adventures of a Bric-a-Brac Hunter. By
Major BYNG HALL.

The Night Side of London. By J. EWING RITCHIE,
author of " About London," &c. New and Enlarged Edition.

The Pilgrim and the Shrine; or Passages from the
Life and Correspondence of Herbert Ainslie, B.A. Cantab. New and
Cheaper Edition, with Corrections and Additions.

Some Habits and Customs of the Working Classes.
By a JOURNEYMAN ENGINEER.

The Great Unwashed. By "THE JOURNEYMAN
ENGINEER." Uniform with " Some Habits and Customs of the
Working Classes."

Town and Country Sketches. By ANDREW HAL-
LIDAY, author of " Sunnyside Papers."

A Course of English Literature. By JAMES HANNAY.
Suitable for Students and Schools.

Modern Characteristics: a Series of Essays from
the " Saturday Review," revised by the Author.

Sunnyside Papers. By ANDREW HALLIDAY, author
of " Everyday Papers," &c.

Essays in Defence of Women. Crown 8vo, hand-
somely bound in cloth, gilt, bevelled boards.

New Edition, revised, of " Everyday Papers."

Everyday Papers. Reprinted from " All the Year
Round," and adapted for Evening Reading at Mechanics' Institutes,
Penny-Reading Clubs, &c. By ANDREW HALLIDAY. 5s.

TINSLEY BROTHERS, 18 CATHERINE STREET, STRAND.

Dutch Pictures. With some Sketches in the Flemish Manner. By GEORGE AUGUSTUS SALA. 5s.

Shooting and Fishing in the Rivers, Prairies, and Backwoods of North America. By B. H. REVOIL. 2 vols. 21s.

Château Frissac; or Home Scenes in France. By the Author of "Photographs of Paris Life." 7s. 6d.

Ten Years in Sarawak. By CHARLES BROOKE, the "Tuanmudah" of Sarawak. With an Introduction by H. H. the Rajah Sir JAMES BROOKE; and numerous Illustrations. 2 vols. 25s.

Dante's Divina Commedia. Translated into English in the Metre and Triple Rhyme of the Original. By Mrs. RAMSAY. 3 vols. 18s.

Abeokuta; and an Exploration of the Cameroons Mountains. By Captain R. F. BURTON, author of "A Pilgrimage to El-Medinah and Meccah," &c. 2 vols., with Portrait of the Author, Map, and Illustrations. 25s.

The Nile Basin. By Captain R. F. BURTON, author of "A Mission to Dahomey." 7s. 6d.

A Mission to Dahomey. Being a Three Months' Residence at the Court of Dahomey. In which are described the Manners and Customs of the Country, including the Human Sacrifice, &c. By Captain R. F. BURTON, late H.M. Commissioner to Dahomey, and the author of "A Pilgrimage to El-Medinah and Meccah." 2 vols., with Illustrations. 25s.

Mornings of the Recess in 1861-4. Being a Series of Literary and Biographical Papers, reprinted and revised from the *Times*, by permission, by the Author. 2 vols. 21s.

The Great Country: Impressions of America. By GEORGE ROSE, M.A. (ARTHUR SKETCHLEY). 8vo, 15s.

A Winter Tour in Spain. By the Author of "Altogether Wrong." 8vo, illustrated, 15s.

TINSLEY BROTHERS, 18 CATHERINE STREET, STRAND.

About London. By J. Ewing Ritchie, author of
"The Night Side of London." 5s.

Fish Hatching; and the Artificial Culture of Fish.
By Frank Buckland. With 5 Illustrations. 5s.

A Bundle of Ballads. Edited by the Author of
"Guy Livingstone." 6s. 6d.

Todleben's Defence of Sebastopol. Being a Review
of General Todleben's Narrative, 1854–5. By William Howard
Russell, LL.D., Special Correspondent of the *Times* during the
Crimean War. 10s. 6d.

Border and Bastille. By the Author of "Guy
Livingstone," "Barren Honour," &c. 10s. 6d.

Masaniello of Naples. By Mrs. Horace St. John.
10s. 6d.

After Breakfast. By George Augustus Sala. 2
vols. 21s.

My Wanderings in West Africa; from Liverpool
to Fernando Po. By a F.R.G.S. 2 vols.

The Battle-fields of 1866. By Edward Dicey,
author of "Rome in 1860," &c. 12s.

Three Hundred Years of a Norman House. With
Genealogical Miscellanies. By James Hannay, author of "A
Course of English Literature," "Satire and Satirists," &c. 12s.

Biographies. and Portraits of some Celebrated
People. By Alphonse de Lamartine. 2 vols. 25s.

The Schleswig-Holstein War. By Edward Dicey,
author of "Rome in 1860." 2 vols. 16s.

From Calcutta to the Snowy Range. By an Old
Indian. With numerous coloured Illustrations. 14s.

TINSLEY BROTHERS, 18 CATHERINE STREET, STRAND.

My Diary in America in the Midst of War. By GEORGE AUGUSTUS SALA. In 2 vols. 8vo, 30s.

Wit and Wisdom from West Africa; or, a Book of Proverbial Philosophy, Idioms, Enigmas, and Laconisms. Compiled by RICHARD F. BURTON, author of "A Mission to Dahomé," "A Pilgrimage to El-Medinah and Meccah," &c. 12s. 6d.

Con Amore; or, Critical Chapters. By JUSTIN McCARTHY, author of "The Waterdale Neighbours." Post 8vo, 12s.

A Saxon's Remedy for Irish Discontent. 9s.

The Law: What I have Seen, What I have Heard, and What I have Known. By CYRUS JAY. 7s. 6d.

Notes and Sketches of the Paris Exhibition. By G. A. SALA, author of "My Diary in America," &c. 8vo, 15s.

Hog Hunting in the East, and other Sports. By Captain J. NEWALL, author of "The Eastern Hunters." With numerous Illustrations. 8vo, 21s.

The Savage-Club Papers. A Volume of Literary and Artistic Contributions, by numerous Authors and Artists of eminence. 12s. Also the Second Series, for 1868. 12s.

The Public Life of Lord Macaulay. By FREDERICK ARNOLD, B.A. of Christ Church, Oxford. Post 8vo, 7s. 6d.

Johnny Robinson: The Story of the Childhood and Schooldays of an "Intelligent Artisan." By the Author of "Some Habits and Customs of the Working Classes." 2 vols. 21s.

The History of Monaco. By H. PEMBERTON. 12s.

TINSLEY BROTHERS, 18 CATHERINE STREET, STRAND.

History of France under the Bourbons, 1589-1830.
By CHARLES DUKE YONGE, Regius Professor, Queen's College, Belfast. In 4 vols. 8vo. Vols. I. and II. contain the Reigns of Henry IV., Louis XIII. and XIV.; Vols. III. and IV. contain the Reigns of Louis XV. and XVI. *3l.*

The Married Life of Anne of Austria, Queen of
France, Mother of Louis XIV.; and the History of Don Sebastian, King of Portugal. Historical Studies. From numerous Unpublished Sources. By MARTHA WALKER FREER. 2 vols. 8vo, 30s.

The Regency of Anne of Austria, Queen of France,
Mother of Louis XIV. From Published and Unpublished Sources. With Portrait. By Miss FREER. 2 vols. 8vo, 30s.

The Eastern Hunters. By Captain JAMES NEWALL.
8vo, with numerous Illustrations. 16s.

From Waterloo to the Peninsula. By G. A. SALA,
author of "My Diary in America," &c. 2 vols. post 8vo, 24s.

The Story of the Diamond Necklace. By HENRY
VIZETELLY. Illustrated with an exact representation of the Diamond Necklace, and a Portrait of the Countess de la Motte, engraved on steel. 2 vols. post 8vo, 25s. Second Edition.

Explorations of the Highlands of the Brazil; with
a full account of the Gold and Diamond Mines; also, Canoeing down Fifteen Hundred Miles of the great River, Sao Francisco, from Sabará to the Sea. By Captain RICHARD F. BURTON, F.R.G.S. &c. In 2 vols. 8vo, with Map and Illustrations, 30s.

The Life of Edmund Kean. From various Published and Original Sources. By F. W. HAWKINS. In 2 vols. 8vo, 30s.

English Photographs. By an American. 8vo, 12s.

The Open Air; or Sketches out of Town. By
JOSEPH VEREY. 1 vol.

British Senators; or Political Sketches, Past and
Present. By J. EWING RITCHIE. Post 8vo, 10s. 6d.

Places and People; being Studies from the Life.
By J. C. PARKINSON. 7s. 6d.

The Life of David Garrick. From Original Family
Papers, and numerous Published and Unpublished Sources. By PERCY FITZGERALD, M.A. 2 vols. 8vo, with Portraits. 36s.

TINSLEY BROTHERS, 18 CATHERINE STREET, STRAND.

TINSLEY BROTHERS'
TWO-SHILLING VOLUMES,
Uniformly bound in Illustrated Wrappers.

To be had at every Railway Stall and of every Bookseller in the Kingdom.

Brakespeare. By the Author of "Guy Livingstone."

The Adventures of Dr. Brady. By W. H. RUSSELL, LL.D.

Not Wisely, but Too Well. By the Author of "Cometh up as a Flower."

Sans Merci. By the Author of "Guy Livingstone."

Maurice Dering. By the same Author.

Recommended to Mercy. By the Author of "Sink or Swim?"

The Rock Ahead. By EDMUND YATES.

The Waterdale Neighbours. By JUSTIN McCARTHY.

The Pretty Widow. By CHARLES H. ROSS.

Miss Forrester. By the Author of "Archie Lovell."

Black Sheep. By EDMUND YATES.

Barren Honour. By the Author of "Guy Livingstone," &c.

Sword and Gown. By the same Author.

The Dower-House. By ANNIE THOMAS.

The Savage-Club Papers (1867). With all the Original Illustrations. Also the Second Series, for 1868.

Every-day Papers. By ANDREW HALLIDAY.

Breaking a Butterfly; or Blanche Ellerslie's Ending. By the Author of "Guy Livingstone."

TINSLEY BROTHERS, 18 CATHERINE STREET, STRAND.

TINSLEY BROTHERS'
CHEAP EDITIONS OF POPULAR NOVELS.

By Mrs. J. H. RIDDELL, author of "George Geith," &c.

Far above Rubies. 6s.	Phemie Keller. 6s.
The Race for Wealth. 6s.	Maxwell Drewitt. 6s.
George Geith. 6s.	Too Much Alone. 6s.
The Rich Husband. 6s.	City and Suburb. 6s.

By Mrs. HENRY WOOD, author of "East Lynne," &c.

Elster's Folly. 6s.	Mildred Arkell. 6s.
St. Martin's Eve. 6s.	Trevlyn Hold. 6s.

By the Author of "Guy Livingstone."

Sword and Gown. 4s. 6d.	Maurice Dering. 6s.
Barren Honour. 6s.	Guy Livingstone. 5s.
Brakespeare. 6s.	Sans Merci. 6s.

Also, now ready, uniform with the above,

Stretton. By HENRY KINGSLEY, author of "Geoffry Hamlyn," &c. 6s.

The Rock Ahead. By EDMUND YATES. 6s.

The Adventures of Dr. Brady. By W. H. RUSSELL, LL.D. 6s.

Black Sheep. By EDMUND YATES, author of "The Rock Ahead," &c. 6s.

Not Wisely, but Too Well. By the Author of "Cometh up as a Flower." 6s.

Lizzie Lorton of Greyrigg. By Mrs. LYNN LINTON, author of "Sowing the Wind," &c. 6s.

Archie Lovell. By the Author of "The Morals of Mayfair," &c. 6s.

Miss Forrester. By the Author of "Archie Lovell," &c. 6s.

Recommended to Mercy. By the Author of "Sink or Swim?" 6s.

TINSLEY BROTHERS, 18 CATHERINE STREET, STRAND.

THE GREAT UNWASHED.

By "The Journeyman Engineer," author of "Some Habits and
Customs of the Working Classes."

" When we say we wish his book could be largely read among his own
class, we do not mean to say that it is only suited to them. It is, as we
think we have shown, a book that everybody ought to read ; for everybody must be anxious to know what sort of folks 'our future masters'
really are."—*Imperial Review.*

" For the second part, which may be regarded as padding introduced
to bring up the publication to the size of an honest volume, we can say
no more than that its light and rather ' scrappy' papers are amusing, and
in no way below the average standard of magazine literature. But
much higher praise is due to the new articles."—*Athenæum.*

" It deals with the working classes, to quote the author, 'in their
public relations, and with the phases of the inner,' or, rather, their
domestic, ' life.' Their relations to the Church and to politics are among
the subjects treated under the first head ; their club-houses, pay-days,
Saturday trading, nightwork, and cheap literature, come under the last."
—*Star.*

" The work is full of valuable information, a considerable portion of
which will be new to those who have not heretofore duly estimated the
importance of acquiring a thorough acquaintance with the habits and
feelings of the majority of their fellow-countrymen."—*The Observer.*

Also, just published, by the same Author, and uniform with the
above, 7s. 6d.

SOME HABITS AND CUSTOMS OF THE WORKING CLASSES.

" Readers who care to know what a spokesman of the working classes
has to say for his order will find this a capital book. The writer
is a clever fellow ; but he is more than that."—*Athenæum.*

" The book is written in a plain, straightforward style, with an entire
absence of humbug. It sets before us a very intelligible picture, and one
which we may assume to be substantially correct, of the manners and
habits of the classes whom he wishes to describe."—*Saturday Review.*

" We are distinctly of opinion that a more just representation of the
working man himself has never appeared in print."—*Pall Mall Gazette.*

" We have here, in a book lately published, a monograph of the
working classes, by one of themselves, which speaks with clear utterance,
neither exaggerating nor extenuating."—*All the Year Round.*

" Professing only to describe some modern characteristics of the
working classes, it fastens on all the most important, and is likely to
throw some useful light on the subject."—*Examiner.*

TINSLEY BROTHERS, 18 CATHERINE STREET, STRAND.

TINSLEY BROTHERS' NEW NOVELS.

George Canterbury's Will. By Mrs. HENRY WOOD,
author of " East Lynne," &c. 3 vols.

Gold and Tinsel. By the Author of "Ups and
Downs of an Old Maid's Life." 3 vols.

Sidney Bellew. A Sporting Story. By FRANCIS
FRANCIS. 2 vols.

Grif; a Story of Australian Life. By B. LEOPOLD
FARJEON. 2 vols.

Not while She Lives. By the Author of " Faithless ; or the Loves of the Period." 2 vols.

A Double Secret and Golden Pippin. By JOHN
POMEROY. 3 vols.

Wee Wifie. By ROSA NOUCHETTE CAREY, author of
" Nellie's Memories." 3 vols.

Oberon Spell. By EDEN ST. LEONARDS. 3 vols.

Martha Planebarke. 3 vols.

Daisie's Dream. By the Author of "Recommended
to Mercy," &c. 3 vols.

Heathfield Hall ; or Prefatory Life. A Youthful
Reminiscence. By HANS SCHREIBER, author of " Nicknames at the
Playingfield College," &c. 10s. 6d.

Phœbe's Mother. By LOUISA ANN MEREDITH,
author of " My Bush Friends in Tasmania." 2 vols.

Beneath the Wheels. By the Author of " Olive
" Varcoe," " Simple as a Dove," &c. 3 vols.

Strong Hands and Steadfast Hearts. By the
Countess von BOTHMER. 3 vols.

The Baronet's Sunbeam. By A. C. W. 3 vols.

Valentine Forde. By CECIL GRIFFITH, author of
" Victory Deane," &c. 3 vols.

TINSLEY BROTHERS, 18 CATHERINE STREET, STRAND.

The Lily and the Rose. By G. H. HARWOOD. 3 vols.

Love Stories of the English Watering-Places. 3 vols.

My Enemy's Daughter. By JUSTIN McCARTHY, author of "The Waterdale Neighbours," "Paul Massie," &c. 3 vols.

The Crust and the Cake. By the Author of "Occupations of a Retired Life." 3 vols.

A County Family. By the Author of "Lost Sir Massingberd," &c. 3 vols.

The Wyvern Mystery. By J. S. LE FANU, author of "Uncle Silas," "Guy Deverell," "Haunted Lives," &c. 3 vols.

Only a Woman's Love. By the EARL OF DESART. 2 vols.

A Perfect Treasure. 1 vol.

Up and Down the World. By the Author of "Never—for Ever." 3 vols.

Lost Footsteps. By JOSEPH VEREY. 3 vols.

The Gage of Honour. By Captain J. T. NEWALL. 3 vols.

Nevermore; or Burnt Butterflies. By JOHN GAUNT. 2 vols.

Twice Refused. By CHARLES E. STIRLING. 2 vols.

Simple as a Dove. By the Author of "Olive Varcoe." 3 vols.

Netherton-on-Sea: a Story. 3 vols.

Found Dead. By the Author of "Lost Sir Massingberd."

Fatal Zero. By the Author of "Polly," &c. 2 vols.

Stretton. By HENRY KINGSLEY, author of "Geoffry Hamlyn," &c. 3 vols.

TINSLEY BROTHERS, 18 CATHERINE STREET, STRAND.

False Colours. By ANNIE THOMAS (Mrs. PENDER CUDLIP), author of "Denis Donne." 3 vols.

The Girl he Married. By JAMES GRANT, author of "The Romance of War," "First Love and Last Love," &c. 3 vols.

In Silk Attire. By WILLIAM BLACK, author of "Love or Marriage." 3 vols. Second Edition.

All but Lost. By G. A. HENTY, author of "The March to Magdala." 3 vols.

A London Romance. By CHARLES H. Ross. 3 vols.

Home from India. By JOHN POMEROY. 2 vols.

The Town-Talk of Clyda. By the Author of "One Foot in the Grave." 3 vols.

John Twiller: a Romance of the Heart. By D. STARKEY, LL.D. 1 vol.

Equal to Either Fortune. A Novel. By the Author of "A Man of Mark," &c. 3 vols.

Under Lock and Key. A Novel. By THOMAS SPEIGHT, author of "Brought to Light," &c. 3 vols.

The Doctor of Beauweir. By WILLIAM GILBERT, author of "Shirley Hall Asylum," "Dr. Austin's Guests," &c. &c. 2 vols.

Mad: a Story of Dust and Ashes. By GEORGE MANVILLE FENN, author of "Bent, not Broken." 3 vols.

Buried Alone. A Story. By a New Writer. 1 vol.

Strange Work. By THOMAS ARCHER. 3 vols.

Nellie's Memories: a Domestic Story. By ROSA NOUCHETTE CAREY. 3 vols.

Clarissa. A Novel. By SAMUEL RICHARDSON. Edited by E. S. DALLAS, author of "The Gay Science," &c. 3 vols.

TINSLEY BROTHERS, 18 CATHERINE STREET, STRAND.

Haunted Lives. By J. S. LE FANU. 3 vols.

Anne Hereford. By Mrs. HENRY WOOD, author
of " East Lynne," &c. 3 vols.

Love or Marriage ? By WILLIAM BLACK. 3 vols.

John Haller's Niece. By the Author of " Never—
for Ever." 3 vols.

Neighbours and Friends. By the Hon. Mrs. HENRY
WEYLAND CHETWYND, author of " Three Hundred a Year." 3 vols.

Martyrs to Fashion. By JOSEPH VEREY. 3 vols.

A House of Cards. By Mrs. CASHEL HOEY. 3 vols.

The Moonstone. By WILKIE COLLINS, author of
" The Woman in White." 3 vols. Second Edition.

Out of the Meshes. A Story. In 3 vols.

Diana Gay. By PERCY FITZGERALD. 3 vols.

The Red Court Farm. By Mrs. HENRY WOOD,
author of " East Lynne," " Trevlyn Hold," &c. 3 vols.

The Two Rubies. By the Author of " Recommended to Mercy," &c. 3 vols.

Wild as a Hawk. By Mrs. MACQUOID, author of
" Hester Kirton," &c. 3 vols.

The Seaboard Parish. By GEORGE MAC DONALD,
author of " Alec Forbes of Howglen," &c. 3 vols.

The Occupations of a Retired Life. By EDWARD
GARRETT. 3 vols.

The Lost Link. By TOM HOOD, author of " A
Golden Heart," &c. 3 vols.

Francesca's Love. By Mrs. EDWARD PULLEYNE. 3
vols.

The Dear Girl. By PERCY FITZGERALD, author of
" Never Forgotten," " Seventy-five Brooke-street," &c. 3 vols.

TINSLEY BROTHERS, 18 CATHERINE STREET, STRAND.

Sink or Swim ? By the Author of "Recommended to Mercy," &c. 3 vols.

High Stakes. By ANNIE THOMAS (Mrs. PENDER CUDLIP), author of "Called to Account." 3 vols.

Only to be Married. By Mrs. FLORENCE WILLIAMSON, author of "Frederick Rivers," &c. 3 vols.

Giant Despair. By MORLEY FARROW. 3 vols.

The Tenants of Malory. By J. S. LE FANU, author of "Uncle Silas," "The House by the Churchyard," &c. &c. 3 vols.

A Search for a Secret. By G. A. HENTY. 3 vols.

Polly : a Village Portrait. 2 vols.

A Golden Heart. By TOM HOOD. 3 vols.

Sowing the Wind. By Mrs. E. LYNN LINTON, author of "Lizzie Lorton of Greyrigg," &c. 3 vols.

Called to Account. By ANNIE THOMAS, author of "Denis Donne," "Sir Victor's Choice," &c. 3 vols.

The Tallants of Barton. By JOSEPH HATTON, author of "Bitter Sweets," &c. 3 vols.

Webs in the Way. By GEORGE MANVILLE FENN, author of "Bent, not Broken," &c. 3 vols.

Hidden Fire. 3 vols.

Taken upon Trust. By the Author of "Recommended to Mercy," &c. 3 vols.

The Second Mrs. Tillotson. By PERCY FITZGERALD, author of "Bella Donna," "Jenny Bell," &c. 3 vols.

The Old Ledger. By G. L. M. STRAUSS. 3 vols.

What Money Can't Do. By the Author of "Altogether Wrong." 3 vols.

One Against the World. By the Author of "Abel Drake's Wife," &c. 3 vols.

Bitter Sweets. A Love Story. By JOSEPH HATTON. 3 vols.

TINSLEY BROTHERS, 18 CATHERINE STREET, STRAND.

Weighed in the Balance. By James A. St. John.
3 vols.

Irkdale : a Lancashire Story. By Benjamin
Brierley. 2 vols.

A Woman's Way. By the Author of " The Field
of Life." 3 vols.

John Neville : Soldier, Sportsman, and Gentleman.
By Captain Newall. 2 vols.

Dacia Singleton. By the Author of " What Money
Can't Do," " Altogether Wrong," &c. 3 vols.

Bent, not Broken. By George Manville Fenn.
3 vols.

Carleton Grange. By the Author of " Abbot's
Cleve." 3 vols.

Three Hundred a Year. By the Hon. Mrs. Henry
Weyland Chetwynd. 2 vols.

Hazel Combe; or, the Golden Rule. By the Au-
thor of " Recommended to Mercy," " Taken upon Trust," &c.3 vols.

Captain Jack; or, the Great Van Brock Property.
By James A. Maitland. 2 vols.

Breaking a Butterfly; or Blanche Ellerslie's Ending.
By the Author of " Guy Livingstone," &c. 3 vols.

Seventy-five Brooke Street. By Percy Fitzgerald, author of " The Second Mrs. Tillotson," 3 vols.

The Forlorn Hope. By Edmund Yates, author of
" Black Sheep," "Kissing the Rod," &c. 3 vols.   .

The Clives of Burcot. By Hesba Stretton, author
of " The Travelling Post-Office" in " Mugby Junction." 3 vols.

More than a Match. By the Author of " Recommended to Mercy," &c. 3 vols.

TINSLEY BROTHERS, 18 CATHERINE STREET, STRAND.

www.ingramcontent.com/pod-product-compliance
Lightning Source LLC
Chambersburg PA
CBHW031344020726
47499CB00005B/1395